REAPER'S WOLVES

MOUNTAIN MC

I0619499

ALASKA'S LADY

HALLIE BENNETT

ALASKA'S LADY

REAPER'S WOLVES MOUNTAIN MC
#2

HALLIE BENNETT

Copyright © 2023 by Hallie Bennett

All rights reserved.
No part of this publication may be reproduced, distributed, or transmitted in any form or by any means, including photocopying, recording, or other electronic or mechanical methods, without the prior written permission of the publisher, except as permitted by U.S. copyright law. For permission requests, contact thearrowedheart@gmail.com. The story, all names, characters, and incidents portrayed in this production are fictitious. No identification with actual persons (living or deceased), places, buildings, and products is intended or should be inferred.

Searching for more mountain men? Check out the introduction to Suitor's Crossing and heart sparks in the Mountain Men of Suitor's Crossing series!

CHAPTER ONE

FAITH

I'm silent—a church mouse trapped in a hell of my own making.

It wasn't supposed to be this way. The preacher's daughter caught in the crossfire between two rival motorcycle clubs, yet the lethal tension suffocating the room couldn't be ignored. Or escaped.

"We need to leave," Kelsey hisses from across the table. We're in a booth at the back of the bar, slightly separated from the stand-off occurring in the middle of the dance floor after a member of the Runners Ridge MC shoved a Ghost Rider.

Everything escalated quickly from there.

Is this what happens at The Ole Aces every night?

Known as a popular hangout for the Reaper's Wolves MC, a biker group who settled at the edge of Suitor's Crossing a few years ago, I've heard whispers of brawls breaking out over women and perceived insults.

My father's sermon last Sunday about resisting the devil's snare—as if riding a motorcycle and wearing leather condemned you to hell—echoes in my mind.

Just my luck that a mini-vacation to Seattle would land me in the middle of another MC club's troubles. Who knew there were so many around?

"Faith? Come on. We need to sneak out before fists start flying and the cops show up."

Kelsey tugs on my arm to get me moving, but I'm stuck, riveted to the scene before me. I knew it was a bad idea to come here tonight. Or really any night.

Bars aren't my scene—nothing is as a preacher's kid.

But I wanted to take a risk, escape my protective bubble.

All my life I've followed the rules and been a good daughter—a good girl. I always consider how my actions will look to our church's congregation. How my words will reflect on my father. Especially after my mother died young, leaving me as her stand-in for matriarchal figure in the church.

It's exhausting and stressful, and I've been doing it for so long that sometimes I'm not even sure which part's an act and which is actually me. I wonder who I really am.

As a twenty-eight-year-old woman, it's not a good feeling questioning your identity, fearing you've wasted years of your life trying to appear perfect.

That's why I booked this getaway to Seattle. To experience a break from the judging eyes of High Ridge. It's a small mountain town full of kind people, or at least that's what I assume. However, most of my interactions are with our church's congregants, and they're... less than friendly, despite my stature as the preacher's daughter.

This weekend was supposed to give me a taste of freedom.

I was going to make a new friend in Kelsey, who I've been chatting with after connecting over Bumble's friend option, and broaden my horizons. Unfortunately, I wasn't expecting them to expand so far past my comfort zone that now we've ventured into a potential biker brawl.

I should've known when Kelsey suggested this place to meet that it was a bad omen. No Man's Land. It even sounded ominous.

But it also felt like my father was speaking and not me. So I came.

Our table bumps into my belly as Kelsey abandons the booth in favor of the hall to our right leading to restrooms and presumably another exit. I tell myself to follow her—will my feet to move—but I can't.

I'm frozen.

A church mouse about to be swallowed whole as punches erupt amongst the shouting and all hell breaks loose.

Glass shatters as empty beer bottles slam across men's heads. Wood cracks under the force of chairs and tables being indiscriminately thrown. It's a madhouse of activity, and I can't tear my gaze away from the unfamiliar sight.

Never in my life have I seen men behaving so violently—rage pouring from their muscular bodies. The guys at church are always so respectful, in control of their actions. They don't fall prey to their "animal lusts" as my father would say.

At least not publicly.

Honestly, they're pretty boring, especially compared to these men.

A stray beer bottle whizzes by my ear before exploding on the wall, and I flinch at the close call. I've got to get out of here. If I return home with an injury, Dad will never let me leave High Ridge alone again.

Suddenly, a calloused palm appears in my line of vision and a gruff voice snaps the thrall the fight has on me—the deep tone far more intriguing.

"Come on, princess. I'm getting you out of here."

CHAPTER TWO

ALASKA

The ride from Anchorage to Seattle has been brutal.
Two weeks on the road and I've forgotten how rough it could be. It's been six months since I got out of the army, but apparently that's long enough to forget how to sleep at odd hours or bunk down on hard ground.

Sure, the scenery is beautiful—full of majestic mountains with snow-crested tops and green pine trees—but I'm happy to finally be within a couple hours to my destination. A quick stop for a bite to eat, then I'll be on the road to Suitor's Crossing—meeting up with the Reaper's Wolves MC, guys I haven't seen in awhile, and dealing with the fallout of my asshole dad betraying the club.

I still can't believe it.

When President Snow called to fill me in on the latest club news, a bark of disbelief couldn't be stifled.

Dad's always been a bastard. But orchestrating thefts of club businesses?

I thought even *he* had a line he wouldn't cross. Once again, good ole dad's proven me wrong.

Which is why I've been sipping on my mug of beer for way longer than necessary before driving straight into whatever awaits me at the club compound.

No Man's Land is exactly as I remember it. Smoky, dingy, and a popular hangout for the local biker crews. Unfortunately, that means it also draws its fair share of trouble.

Because just as I'm about to drop a tip on the table and leave for the final stretch of my journey, a fucking fight breaks out between two assholes on the dance floor.

I'm about to sidestep the brewing trouble and exit the bar, except I see *her*—the curvy little princess in the back booth, her eyes wide as she watches the scene of men punching each other and trashing the place.

She's alone, which has my protective instincts immediately rising to the forefront.

What the hell is she doing here?

Honey blonde hair rests in loose waves over her shoulders, and lush tits swell over the modest neckline of her dress. A woman like her is too pure, too good for a place like this—a fucking lady.

Someone sends a beer bottle flying far too close to her delicate face for my liking, and a growl of anger rumbles from my chest. I've got to get this innocent girl out of here before she gets hurt. Especially since she resembles a deer in headlights amongst the chaos.

Marching across the bar floor, avoiding punches and flying furniture, I hold my hand out for her. "Come on, princess. I'm getting you out of here."

Violet eyes peer up at me and my heart stops. Surely, those can't be real, right? No one has eyes the color of lavender in real life.

Without a word, her soft palm cautiously slides into mine, kickstarting my pulse into a galloping steel horse. Sparks shoot up my arm as I squeeze her fingers tight then pull her behind me. We hurry toward the back exit of the bar without incident, and the breath of fresh air is a welcome reprieve from the sweaty, smoky mess of indoors.

Not to mention it's clearing the clouds in my head after rescuing this pretty little princess.

Our footsteps crunch over the gravel parking lot until we reach my bike. Her hand's still in mine, my giant bearpaw engulfing her delicate palm. I should release her. She's out of harm's way. Safe. But my body refuses to listen to reason and opts to stroke her soft skin with my thumb instead.

"Are you okay?" I peer down into those mesmerizing pools of violet. Thick lashes frame their beauty like a Monet painting gilded in gold to perfectly display its artistry.

What the fuck?

Monet? Artistry? I'm turning into a damned poet because of one curvy woman.

"Yes, thank you..." Moonlight shines on her cheeks, highlighting a flush of pink rising to the forefront. "I don't know what happened. I just kind of froze. Pretty stupid, huh?"

A frown tugs on my mouth. "Not stupid. Understandable. You've probably never witnessed something like that, right?"

She shakes her head. "No, but common sense says to run."

"Common sense says to assess the situation and figure out the best course of action. Your mind was just working through the next steps when I showed up. No shame in that."

A surprised laugh bursts out, and her smile warms my chest, puffs it out in pride knowing I made her feel a little better.

"I appreciate the vote of confidence in my instincts," she says before tucking a wave of blonde behind her ear. "I'm Faith, by the way."

"Alaska," I gave her my club name.

"That's unique."

I shrug. "Not really. I spend a lot of time in Alaska, so the club figured it fit."

Faith's brows lift in question. "Club? Like those guys inside?" She jerks a thumb toward No Man's Land where shouts of anger could still be heard from out here.

"I'd like to think we're not as rowdy, but yeah... I'm part of the Reaper's Wolves MC. That's actually where I'm headed. Suitor's Crossing to meet back up with the club." Though I really don't feel like abandoning Faith to deal with club business.

Especially business that involves Snake, my good for nothing dad.

"Do you need a ride home?" I ask, surveying the parking lot and only seeing a sea of motorcycles. No way she rode in on one of those.

"I do, but I don't want to put you out. You've already helped me once tonight. I'll just call an Uber or something." She bites her lip and tries to retreat, but my fingers gently squeeze hers, refusing to let her go so easily.

"Not a chance in hell," I growl. Shock stiffens her features at my harsh tone, and I immediately try to rein in the possessive decree, striving for congeniality despite never being described as congenial in my life. "It's late and who knows when an Uber will get here. It's safer if I drive you home. Trust me."

Trust me to keep you safe.

Trust me to give you what you need.
Trust me to make you come—

Seriously, what the hell? I barely know Faith, but all sorts of barbaric fantasies are riddling my body with need. My cock's a fucking lead pipe pressing against the zipper of my jeans.

She's not mine.

Not my woman.

Too bad the desire in my veins didn't get the memo.

CHAPTER THREE

FAITH

My period must be about to start.

What other explanation can there be for why my body is aching to be taken? My hormones are raging and all it wants is to be fucked. Even thinking the word makes me cringe.

I don't curse.

But I can't call it anything else. It just fits.

Raw. Rough. Taken by this giant biker.

He rescued me like a knight in shining armor, so he can't be that bad, right? I certainly can't judge him for being at the bar when I was there, too.

When Alaska appeared, his large palm reaching out for mine, the ice freezing me in place during the brawl melted like snow cones on summer day. I felt hot, fluid—or at least, the arousal that centered in my pussy did. It was like all my daydreams convalesced into one perfect moment where I was seen. Cared for. Protected.

Alaska's motorcycle rumbles to a stop in front of the hotel I'm staying at, disrupting my wayward thoughts. I still can't believe I agreed to riding on the back of a stranger's bike. Carefully dismounting, my legs tremble from straddling such a monstrous piece of metal and the burly biker who controlled it.

God, he'd felt good. Firm muscles flexing with each turn. Solid strength beneath my embrace as I held on for dear life as we zoomed back to the city.

Alaska helps me out of the helmet before removing his own, shaking out his shaggy hair. "Are you doing alright?" he asks, that gruff tone shooting straight to my core.

"I... I'm fine," I stutter, biting my lip, unsure of what to do next.

That's a lie. I know what I *want* to do next. The question is whether or not I'll be brave enough.

This is your one shot.

Your mind wants it.

Your body needs it.

Licking my lips, I swallow past the lump in my throat and blurt out, "Would you like to come up to my room?"

Alaska stiffens in front of me, becoming a stony boulder. Solid and craggy. Ready to crush you at a moment's notice.

"Is that what you want, princess?" His head tilts to the side as if to study my resolve. Dark eyes probe my own, searching for confirmation.

I shudder at the nickname. Enjoy the way it makes me feel small and protected. "Yes," I say and hold out my hand for him to take. As if I offer myself to wild bikers every night.

Five minutes later, we're at my hotel room, and I slide the key card into the slot, waiting for the light to turn green before pushing inside. When the door shuts, I hear the turn of the lock, and butterflies take flight in my belly.

Heat engulfs my back as Alaska wraps his muscular arms around me, drawing me into his firm chest. It's like he's this powerful growly bear, and I'm a tiny rabbit at the mercy of his big paws.

That image shouldn't turn me on as much as it does.

"Do you know what you're asking by inviting me to your room like this?" His hot breath hits my ear, his fingers tugging one of my sleeves down over my shoulder to expose the skin.

"I want you to..." *Can I say it? Should I say it?* "Fuck me."

The two words come out quiet and shy. Embarrassment flushes my skin red, and I want to hide from him. I'm sure the women in his past have been more confident in what they asked for, but this is my first attempt at doing what I want, at grabbing a little bit of freedom for myself.

Who can blame me for being nervous?

"Goddamn," he mutters under his breath. I swear he shudders behind me, but that can't be right. Why would he be anxious? "Don't worry, princess, I'll fuck that sweet little pussy of yours real good. Tomorrow you're gonna be sore and aching after my big cock stretches out that cunt of yours."

I whimper at the promise, rubbing my thighs together. God, I want that so desperately. "Touch me, please," a pleading note enters my voice.

One of his hands strokes down my side to slide beneath my dress. It's shorter than I usually wear. New and specifically bought for this vacation. It never occurred to me that it'd be the perfect length for a man to easily venture under to slip between my thighs and cup my panty-covered pussy.

Alaska squeezes the soft flesh and groans.

"Already wet for me? Did you like riding on the back of my bike, princess? Feeling all that power between your thighs? Cradling me with your body? Soon you're gonna be doing it again, but on your back as I fill you up with my thick cock. Driving deep so you know how a man claims his woman."

Swallowing hard, I imagine what it would be like to be Alaska's woman.

So caveman-like to be owned by a man like him.

But strangely I desire it. For some reason it feels different and right.

My father would probably say *he* owns me. I'm his property as his daughter and him being the head of the household. But with Alaska, being his property would mean something entirely different. Something better.

Rough fingertips ease under my panties to separate my wet folds. He grazes my clitoris before plunging into my clenching channel, and it's a shock to feel the sudden fullness, though not unwelcome.

Especially when his other hand massages my breast before snaking beneath the neckline of my dress to pinch my nipple through the lace bra.

"I'm gonna enjoy this, princess. Fucking this soaking cunt, sucking on these puffy nipples. These sweet tits are aching to be loved by a big man like me," he croons, milking my nipple as his fingers thrust in and out of me with slow deliberation. "You're just curvy all over, aren't you?"

The approval in his voice warms me from the inside out. Dad still makes comments about my weight, comments that sting to hear. Alaska's approval, his lust for my body is a soothing balm for a wound that's festered for years, if not decades.

"Please don't hold back. I want everything," I say. Writhing in his embrace, I cover his hands with mine, urging him to take what he wants from me. Full permission given.

"You think you can handle that?" He nips my neck with his teeth, and his beard scrapes along my nerve endings. What would it feel like between my thighs? Scraping across my clit?

"I'm going to try," I promise.

"Brave little princess," he muses. Suddenly, he releases me, and I find myself face forward on the mattress, Alaska's hand at the small of my back holding me down.

"Lay just like this," he commands. Clothing rustles in the background—the clink of his belt coming undone, the whisper of a zipper being lowered.

Anticipation heightens my arousal, and I can't help but work my knees under me so I can arch into his touch.

"There's a good girl." His palm rubs circles over my back then lower to massage my bottom. "Already preparing for your man's possession, presenting that juicy ass of yours to me."

Preachers' daughters don't act this way.

They don't arch into a biker's coarse palms with lust. They don't pant in excitement for a man's dominant possession. Yet here I am doing all of these things, forgetting all those lessons about purity—about waiting for marriage.

All those strict rules about keeping myself innocent, a virgin only for my husband.

If only my father knew.

The bed dips behind me before a shadow falls across the bed, Alaska's larger body blanketing me in warmth. His arms cage me in while his erection nestles against my butt. The wiry hair on his chest brushes my back, and I've never felt more aware of my femininity because Alaska makes me feel delicate. Precious. Tiny.

And compared to him, I suppose I am.

"Ever have a man between these thick thighs of yours?" he asks. His teeth rake down the side of my neck before latching onto my shoulder and sucking hard.

He's leaving his mark, and oh, how I wish I could let people see it after tonight. Unfortunately, it will be efficiently hidden behind makeup if there's anything I can do about it. My father and the rest of the church staff would have a conniption fit if I walked into the church office Monday morning with a love bite showing.

"No, I'm a virgin," I admit, praying my inexperience doesn't turn him off.

An animalistic growl shoots another burst of arousal down my spine. "An innocent little virgin, huh?" Alaska presses a kiss to the center of my back, working his way lower, following each vertebrae, until he reaches the top of my bottom and his hands part the cheeks.

Surely, he isn't...

But the thought goes unfinished as his tongue dives lower and plunges straight into my pussy.

"Oh god," I cry out. The dexterous muscle licks along my inner walls before retreating, and then thrusting again.

"Goddamn, this pussy is sweet. A virgin cherry," he rumbles. "Just for me."

Two fingers capture my clit and tease the sensitive flesh to even higher heights. Hungry sounds vibrate behind me as my hands clutch the bedsheets, my hips rocking backward to feel more of his mouth on me.

His lips, his tongue, his beard. They all create a fire in the pit of my stomach, one that's threatening to explode and burn me from fingertips to toes. God, how I want to be burned.

I feel like I've been living frozen for years, and this is the first time I've been awakened. My father likes to preach in the pulpit about the downfalls of being a *lukewarm Christian*, but I feel like I've been a lukewarm woman.

Except Alaska's flipping the switch, lighting me on fire from the inside out.

And I love it.

SHAME SLAMS INTO ME first thing the next morning. Alaska's muscular arm is wrapped around my waist as he spoons me from behind, and everything from last night replays in my mind.

The things I did.

The things I asked for.

Guilt is a heavy blow to the satisfaction I felt at the time.

Tempering my breathing, I slowly slip out of bed and blink away tears. Inside there's a war going on. I'm torn between loving and hating what I did.

Dragging on my clothes, I tiptoe around the room to gather my things before sneaking out of the room like a coward. But I can't face Alaska again. Can't hear him try to awkwardly extract himself from whatever last night was. Can't witness the relegation of last night to a simple one-night stand.

I was a virgin, I didn't want to be, and now I'm not.

Except there's an unexpected pain that comes with the knowledge.

Because no matter how much I disagree with my dad's teachings about purity and innocence—I know God loves me the way I am and nothing will change that, thank you very much—the romantic side of me always equated saving myself for my husband as this "soulmates" kind of act.

Where he and I were the only ones for each other—true love. However naive the fantasy had been.

Now that'll never happen because I gave myself to a stranger.

A man I'll never see again, who only cared enough about me last night to fuck me.

The realization brings a fresh wave of tears as I jump into my car and leave the parking lot.

Cry it out now, but then you need to buck up before getting home.

I don't want my dad noticing any signs of distress. Don't want to field awkward questions when he's already going to demand a full rundown of my weekend—of the who, what, and where.

Following signs for a park, I pull into the sparse lot and park under a shady tree, hoping it will shield me from onlookers as I rest my forehead on the wheel and give in to the tears.

I don't blame Alaska for anything. He figured I was a typical woman who knew the score. And I did. *Do.* It's my ultra-conservative upbringing that's the problem.

I pray this guilty phase won't last long, and I can go back to being deliriously happy and proud about doing something for myself. Because it had been wonderful. Life-altering.

Alaska had been generous, an unselfish lover. He'd made me feel secure despite my lack of experience.

And yet... There's a niggling doubt that last night's epic passion will always be shared with an equally hefty load of shame and sadness.

CHAPTER FOUR

ALASKA

The scent of roses tickles my nose as I stretch an arm across the bed searching for Faith. Last night was incredible, and Faith was unlike any virgin I'd ever heard of.

Wild and willing for whatever I wanted. Sweet and giving at every turn.

My little princess was made for me.

I just can't believe how lucky I was to find her at No Man's Land of all places.

Discovering the bed cold beneath my palm, I blink away the sleep in my eyes and look around the room, my gut clenching at the absence of Faith's belongings—her strewn clothes and a purple suitcase.

"Faith?" I call out, hoping she's just in the bathroom.

No answer.

"Faith!" I say, louder this time.

Again, silence.

"Fuck!" Tossing the covers aside, I snag my jeans and pull them on, quickly dressing and searching the room, growling when I don't find any sign of her.

She fucking left me. Snuck away without my knowledge.

Damn, six months out of the military really *has* screwed me over if I didn't even notice my dream girl deserting me. Though in my defense, I've never had pussy that good.

Faith knocked me out last night with her endless passion—that combined with the long journey I've nearly completed. But if she thinks she can escape me so easily, she's got another thing coming.

Because somewhere between No Man's land and Faith's hotel last night, I decided to fuck the consequences. Fuck the illogical nature of my desire. Faith was my woman—something I never thought I'd crave so desperately.

Racing out of the hotel room, I hop on my bike and rev the engine before peeling out of the parking lot, heading straight for Suitor's Crossing. A threadbare plan forms in my mind while I drive. One where our tech guy, Ollie, hacks into the hotel's reservation list to discover Faith's identity.

Should've gotten her last name before fucking her.

But collecting information was the furthest thing from my mind yesterday. I was too focused on kissing her pretty bow mouth, caressing her silky skin, feeling the clasp of her pussy on my cock. It never occurred to me that she might bail before we got a chance to talk this morning.

The two-hour drive to Suitor's Crossing flies by as my frustration grows the closer I get to my destination. Frustration and fear. What if I never find Faith again? What if we were destined for one night together, and that's it?

The thought makes me sick to my stomach.

Pulling into the Reaper's Wolves compound, I park my bike and stomp into the clubhouse, ignoring the surprised greetings from members gathered around the big screen TV watching football. I'm on a mission that doesn't include shooting the breeze with men I haven't seen in forever.

The need to find my girl consumes me.

Ollie's where I expected him to be in the back of the clubhouse with tons of computers set up around him. As the club's tech man, he gathers information like a squirrel storing nuts. I don't know how he does it, but if anyone can help me find Faith, it's him.

"Hey man," I say, plopping into a rolling desk chair beside him.

"Alaska, dude, I wasn't expecting you today. Does Prez know you're here?"

"Not yet. You're my first stop."

"To what do I owe the pleasure?" He smirks before returning to typing something on a green LED-lit keyboard.

"I need you to hack into a hotel's reservations list and find a guest for me."

Ollie snorts and shakes his head. "You know that's illegal, right? We're not that kind of MC, remember?"

"No shit. My dad got kicked out because of it." Not that I disagree with the decision, but I don't need a smartass answer. I need to know how to find Faith again.

"Sorry." Ollie quickly sobers. "Didn't mean to insinuate—"

I raise my hand to stop his explanation. "I know." Ollie was the one who figured out my dad was the rat in the club who'd been helping a rival MC rob our businesses. There's no hard feelings—he was just doing his job—but maybe I can use his guilt to my advantage.

When it comes to my princess, I'm not above getting down and dirty.

"Why don't you make it up to me by learning about the guest staying in room 211 last night? That's all I need. In the grand scheme of law-breaking, surely, that's not a big deal. It's just a name."

"Does this have to do with your dad? Did you hear he's staying there or something?" Ollie asks, punching a few more buttons into the computer. A white tab pops up before filling with lines of black code.

"No, I don't know where the fuck he is." And I don't care.

Ollie shrugs. "Well, unfortunately, I'm busy working on a project for Prez. Maybe I'll be able to help you afterwards once you get his permission, since you'll be putting the club at risk."

"Don't act like you're a teenager cracking your first security system," I scoff. "There's no risk when you won't get caught. Besides, I need the information now."

"Until you get the okay from Prez, my hands are tied." He doesn't sound very broken up about it, just keeps typing away, effectively dismissing me.

"Seriously?"

"You know how to track somebody. Find them yourself."

"Fuck you, too, then," I say, flipping him the bird and stomping out of the room. This is what I get for not being at the club full-time. I don't hold much weight with the guys since I'm not around twenty-four-seven.

Makes it easier for them to turn down requests.

It's annoying as hell.

ONE FUCKING WEEK.

That's how long it's been since I found—*and lost*—Faith.

Snow, president of the Reaper's Wolves MC, denied my request for Ollie to break into the hotel's system, citing the trouble the club just overcame with my dad and some cops in Everton.

"We need to remain above board now more than ever," he'd said.

Except if it was *his* woman who went missing, I guarantee he'd change his tune. Snow's obsessed with his Little Owl, and my gut tightens every time I see them together because that should be me and Faith.

Speaking of which, the couple rounds Snow's truck after he helps her down to the gravel church parking lot. We're preparing to attend a Sunday church service in High Ridge, and no, that's not a fucking joke.

The club's been fielding letters of harassment and random congregants banging on the clubhouse door for weeks, and this is Snow's response—to show up at their church to prove we're not the heathens bent for hell they think we are. He's gotten it into his head that we just need to have a civil conversation with the preacher after the service to clear the air.

I'm not so sure.

The world's full of rabid fanatics intent on using the Lord's name to further their cause. Spouting God's support for whatever agenda they have. I doubt reason will get through to people who've decided we're a band of devil worshippers without even knowing us.

"Remember to stay calm and polite. We don't want to give anyone a reason to believe the shit they're accusing us of. Got it?" Snow stares down the six of us he chose to accompany him and his girl, Caroline, to the service.

Grumbled agreements fill the air as we all nod. We're not exactly choir boys, but we'll be good.

Though none of us went as far as Snow and dressed for the occasion—slacks, loafers, and a button down shirt. I like my leather cut, jeans, and scuffed boots just fine, and so does Jesus.

"Alright, let's get this over with. Reverend Harris is over there greeting everyone, so we might as well join the line."

"Good luck, guys. You've got this." Caroline smiles and gives us a thumbs up before looping an arm through Snow's, our fearless leaders charging forward.

I lag behind the group as older couples and families stare agape at our march across the gravel. It's like we're their personal apocalypse—instead of four horsemen, we're seven grizzled men and one lady who rode in on steel horses.

It'd be funny if I wasn't so determined to get back to the clubhouse and continue my search for Faith. I haven't had much luck so far, but when I questioned the bartender at No Man's Land, he mentioned a regular customer who'd been with Faith before abandoning her. Some woman named Kelsey.

If I find her, maybe I can find my princess, too.

I just have to survive this sermon first.

CHAPTER FIVE

FAITH

The dry paper towel scratches across my forehead rather than collect the nervous sweat I'm drenched in. The heavy knit of my sweater dress and thick tights don't help either.

I should be outside greeting church members attending this morning's service, but the moment I heard the rumble of motorcycles enter the parking lot, I freaked out, excusing myself to run inside for a breather.

Thank God for Dad's private bathroom. Otherwise, I'd have to make up an excuse to the old ladies congregated in the public restrooms as to why I'm sweating like a whore in church when it's fifty degrees outside.

If they knew what you did last weekend, the "whore in church" analogy wouldn't be too far off...

We're not judging anymore, remember?

After wallowing in guilt all week, I finally decided enough was enough. There's nothing shameful about what I did, despite my father's voice condemning me in my head.

I'm a grown woman with natural desires, and for once, I allowed myself to experience true pleasure. Like all the heroines in the romance novels I read. It's thanks to them that I'm not traumatized by purity culture and my father's judgment.

Okay, I'm still a little traumatized, but I'm working on it.

Dad never suspected a thing when I used to escape to High Ridge's tiny library every afternoon once school was released. He even bragged about what a studious daughter he had.

Little did he know Ms. Haversham, the librarian, found me lingering around the romance section one day and introduced me to an entire world of passion and acceptance.

I cut my teeth on classics like Kathleen Woodiwiss's *Shanna* and Julie Garwood's *The Wedding*, gobbling up their sweeping stories like a kid in a candy store. Then, when e-books became popular, another world opened to me as newer releases that my library couldn't afford were available.

Good thing Dad can't access my e-reader.

Especially now that I've stuffed it full of sexy bikers because of Alaska.

"Forget about him." A determined reflection glares back at my bent form, my hands clenching the sides of the porcelain sink.

I know it's a losing battle, though. I won't forget Alaska anytime soon, especially when he's become part of my nightly routine—read a chapter or two of my latest biker book then snag my Satisfyer Pro 2, a life-changing air-pulse clit stimulator. My trusty Rabbit was great and all, but after skeptically trying air-pulse technology versus vibration, I was sold.

My pussy dampens, and my thighs clench against the sudden ache. Geez, just thinking about going home after church to pleasure myself with the memory of Alaska is turning me on.

And it's so wrong to use him that way, even if it's just a fantasy.

"Faith, are you finished yet? Beau's almost done with the announcements." My father raps on the bathroom door, jolting me into action.

Patting another paper towel over my forehead and neck, I toss the wadded up sheet in the trashcan before flinging the door open with a forced smile. "Sorry, I wasn't feeling well, but I'm better now."

Dad's palm falls to the center of my back and pushes me forward, practically shoving me toward the closed door that leads into the sanctuary. He clicks his tongue and grunts. "The devil's testing us today. First, you get sick, then those heathens appear. But I won't be silenced. The armor of God protects me and my church; we won't be cowed today," he promises, his voice swelling like it does when he's on the pulpit.

It takes every ounce of self-control not to roll my eyes. The power of speaking Christian-ese is strong with my father.

Jesus loves those "heathens," too, you know!

That's what I want to say, but I'm not about to start a fight with him, especially one I can't win.

Dad ushers me into the sanctuary while everyone's head is bowed for prayer. Keeping my eyes to the ground, I scurry to my usual seat in the front pew and wait for Beau's *amen* before looking up to see my dad standing behind the pulpit. His attention focuses on the rear of the room immediately.

"Friends, we have special guests with us this morning. The Lord is putting our faith to the test, but we won't fail, will we?"

A chorus of "no's" from the congregation rings in the air, and embarrassment causes a new wave of nervous sweat to rise. Is he really going to insult and condemn the bikers while they're actually in attendance?

Great impression we're making... I want to sink into the old seventies era carpet.

I love Jesus, but sometimes it's really difficult to love Christians—even if, technically, I am one. A few enthusiastic outliers like my dad cast a shadow over the rest of us, and it's exhausting and humiliating.

"Sir, sit down!" Dad erupts into angry shouts, his face darkening to an ugly shade of purple. If he doesn't calm down, he's liable to have a heart attack.

Twisting in my seat, I spot the reason for his sudden outburst. A husky man in leather is tromping down the center aisle, and his hardened gaze is focused on me.

Wheezing at the sudden lack of oxygen, one hand goes to my neck, where the mark Alaska left has practically faded to nothingness, while the fingernails of my other hand dig into the wooden pew.

How did he find me?

Is this really happening?

Because my burly, bearded biker is here.

And he doesn't look too happy with me.

CHAPTER SIX

ALASKA

"**I** command you to leave this place. Take your demon brothers with you and begone!"

The pastor continues to rave from his pulpit as I stomp toward my girl. She entered the room at the last minute, but there was no mistaking her sexy curves and that particular shade of blonde hair.

I can't believe my good fortune at finding her. It just sucks that it's in this loony bin. Reverend Harris really thinks he's casting out evil spirits by invoking the Lord's name against me and my club. Clearly, Snow's plan to speak with the man and prove our decency was doomed to fail.

No way this motherfucker listens to reason. Otherwise, he wouldn't still be calling on everyone and their mother to strike me down with a bolt of lightning or some shit.

Faith stares at me with wide eyes as I finally reach her spot at the front of the church. When she first appeared, I contemplated waiting until after the service to approach her, but then my little princess's history of disappearing convinced me that the wisest course of action was to lock her down.

Now.

"I've been looking for you, princess." She flushes at the nickname, and I remember how soft and gooey she went every time I used the term of endearment during our one night together. Frustrated all over again by her ghosting me, I growl, "You left me, but don't think you're getting away again."

I bend down and flip her over my shoulder, making sure the skirt of her dress covers her ass with a quick swat to the fleshy cheek, before hauling her past a crowd of fearful churchgoers.

"Unhand my daughter, you... you..." The reverend sputters behind us. My footsteps don't falter, though I'm reeling from the news that Faith is his fucking daughter!

How could someone so sweet come from that bastard?

Snow meets me at the end of the aisle with Caroline anxiously wringing her hands beside him. The rest of the crew stands behind him in confusion.

"What the fuck is going on? Why are you kidnapping the damn preacher's daughter?" Snow hisses.

"Because she's mine," I snap, continuing my journey outside. The walk to my bike is short, which is a blessing because I'm sure her dad's calling the cops and reporting me for kidnapping.

Not that I give a fuck.

Lowering Faith to her feet, I rummage in the leather bag tied onto the back seat and grab the spare helmet, fitting it over her head.

"What are you doing here? I never thought..."

"No, you didn't," I agree, shaking my head in annoyance. "If you did, then you never would've abandoned me in bed after the best fucking night of my life. You would've been there when I woke up, and you would've been screaming my name as I ate you for breakfast."

"You wanted me to stay?"

"What part of me claiming your sweet little body said otherwise?"

A crowd spills from the church, and it won't be long before we're surrounded by Bible-thumping fanatics intent on rescuing their wayward lamb. One couple is already waving their fists in Timber and Grim's faces as if the giant motherfuckers can't swat them away like two annoying horseflies.

Pointing toward my Harley, I say, "Look, we can do this here in front of your church or we can go somewhere more private. Either way, you're ending up over my knee while I spank that round ass of yours for leaving me."

Faith gasps in shock then glances between me and the group of angry congregants led by her father. Cautiously, she raises the skirt of her dress above her knees and straddles the bike, her spine ramrod straight.

"Take me away."

"Good choice, princess."

Strapping on my helmet, I climb in front of her and rev the bike to life. The powerful growl of the engine blocks out everything except for the heat of Faith and her plush curves molding to my back.

Fuck, I've missed her arms wrapped around my waist, clinging tightly to my body for stability and protection.

Roaring out of the gravel parking lot, we fly down the deserted country road heading toward the Reaper's Wolves compound. I half expect a line of cars to follow, or at least a police vehicle with lights flashing to pull us over, but the drive is blessedly calm and trouble-free.

When we reach the compound, I pass the main house in favor of a clearing at the rear of the property. I don't have a cabin like some of the guys—an oversight that will need to be remedied as soon as possible now that I've got a woman—so it's the best I can do at the moment.

Silence fills the air once I cut the engine.

"So, tell me, princess. Why'd you disappear without a word?" I ask after we've both gotten off the bike and removed our helmets.

Faith avoids eye contact, instead she picks at the leather stitching on the seat and shakes her head. "You wouldn't understand."

"Try me." Crossing my arms over my chest, I wait for her explanation. Not that it will justify her actions, but I need to understand why she left when I could've sworn she felt the same way as me that night.

I'd never experienced such pleasure and soul-deep contentment in my life, and it was all because of her.

When I drove into Suitor's Crossing later that day, a large billboard heralded the town's claim to fame—*heart sparks*. Another name for soul mates, the small town was known for couples finding and recognizing "the one" immediately.

As soon as I saw that sign I knew Faith was my *heart spark*, my one.

Love at first sight never factored into my mind. It sounded like a bunch of bullshit spouted by romantic saps. But I'm a convert now. Guess it really does only take meeting the right person for you to just "know."

Except Faith doesn't seem to have had the same epiphany.

The realization is a punch to the gut.

"You saw my dad. How he views men like you and your friends. I've grown up with his harsh judgments, especially as it pertains to purity and sex." A bark of bitter laughter rises from her. "Do you know how difficult it is to live underneath his domineering shadow for so long? I don't agree with everything he teaches, but those lessons are still buried inside of me."

She spares me a glance, and I reel at the sight of tears gleaming in her beautiful eyes.

"I wanted you that night, Alaska, and I don't regret what we did. But when I woke up that morning, all the shame and guilt of no longer being a virgin hit me like a freaking tidal wave. I was drowning in it. How was I to know I meant more to you than a one night stand? You were my first... *everything*."

Her head drops back as she stares up at the canopy of fall leaves overhead, blinking rapidly as stray tears track across her cheek. "So, I panicked and ran. I'm sorry. I'm sure the other women you've been with never..."

"Hey." My fingers tilt her chin down as I finally give in to the urge to touch her. "There's no comparison. Don't ever think you're less than someone because of how you were raised or because of your inexperience or because of *any-fucking-thing*. Got it?"

I gently shake her. "You are a fucking lady. A hot as hell, curvy as fuck, and sweet as honey princess who has an asshole for a father. I can relate. My dad sucks, too."

Faith bites her lip then reluctantly chuckles, swiping at the tears seeping from under her lashes. "Are you going for a record with the amount of curse words you just used to describe me?" Releasing a deep breath, she steps closer and rests her forehead on my chest.

"Do you forgive me for leaving?" The soft tremor in her voice breaks my heart.

"Of course. I could never stay mad at you for long. But don't think I've forgotten about your punishment." My palm already itches to feel the jiggle of her ass beneath it.

"M... my punishment?" She tries to retreat, but I'm not letting her escape.

Never again.

"That's right, princess." Shifting to straddle my bike for stability, I tug Faith forward until she tumbles over my lap with a yelp, her ass in the air. "If you ever think about leaving me again, I want you to remember this moment because if I have to catch you a second time, I won't be so lenient."

"You call this lenient?" She huffs, wiggling in my grasp. Annoyance filters through the previous sadness blanketing her form, and I'm happy to see the change. I can't stand seeing her in pain. "I'm not a child to be disciplined."

"No, you're my woman who needs a reminder of who she belongs to."

I slide my hand along the inside of her thigh until it reaches the elastic band of her tights. These have got to go. I hate barriers between us, and this one's easy enough to remove.

Maneuvering the fabric lower to rest beneath her plump ass cheeks, I admire the view of her body presented so prettily for me. Damn, she even makes thick tights sexy.

"We barely know each other..." Her breath hitches in her lungs as I give her a test swat to the left cheek. "You can't just claim a person."

"I'm not. I'm claiming *you*."

Smack!

The slap of my palm on her ass resounds in the quiet forest. Light pink blooms on the pale flesh, and I'm mesmerized by the change.

It needs a twin.

Smack!

A matching pat to her other cheek follows.

"Alaska..." Faith moans my name in the sexiest little drawl. Her fingers grab onto my bike and my leg, her manicured nails digging into the denim.

"Nolan," I correct. "To you, I'm Nolan. Alaska's my club name."

Smack!

After a few more minutes, her ass is a fiery red that burns to the touch, but I love seeing the outline of my palm branding her body. My fingers slide between her thighs to test her response to the spanking, and immediately a curse of aroused wonder spills out.

My girl is fucking soaked.

"You're so wet, princess. You needed this, didn't you? Needed your man to prove his ownership. Don't worry, I won't let you doubt my commitment ever again." Petting her pussy, I circle her clit before plunging into her hot channel.

"Oh, god... We shouldn't be doing this out here," she pants, though her pussy clenches around me in direct contrast to her words. "Anyone could see us."

"We're all alone, princess. My club brothers are either sleeping at the main house or still dealing with the mess we left at your church. No one is going to see us. No one is going to hear us, so make sure you give me every one of those breathy moans and shouts of pleasure I've been missing."

I twist my fingers to hit the spongy spot deep inside her cunt and grunt at the gush of cream that swiftly coats my hand. Yeah, Faith is a dirty girl, even if she won't admit it aloud.

A lady in the streets and a freak in the sheets. Or over my bike as it stands.

I cup the back of her neck with my free hand and enjoy the twitch of her muscles at the contact. It's possessive as fuck, but I can't resist the rough desire that overcomes me whenever I'm near her.

I want Faith and everyone within a hundred mile radius to know she's mine.

If another man even thinks about stealing her away, they'll get a fucking bullet in the head. Wouldn't be the first bastard I've killed. It's what sniper training taught me.

"Nolan... Please..." She's close, her body's wound tight with tension, just waiting for me to push her over the edge.

"I'm here, baby. Just let go. Give me that sweet orgasm your body's begging to release." Withdrawing my hand from her pussy, I spank her ass again—*one, two, three*—before dropping to her clit and milking the throbbing little button until Faith cries out and shudders on my lap.

Another rush of warmth drips down my hand as she comes, and I groan in satisfaction, determined to wring her cunt of every last drop of pleasure.

When Faith collapses with a heavy sigh, I gently readjust her body so she sits sideways on my lap, her head resting under my chin. Her legs are awkwardly clamped together by her tights, but otherwise, she's comfortable, sinking into me as I try to get my hard cock under control.

It demands attention. Yearns to be squeezed by my girl's tight pussy.

But it's just gonna have to wait, because the next time I fuck Faith with my cock, we're going to be in my bed, and she's going to be tied to the bedpost to guarantee she stays put.

I don't care if that makes me sound like a caveman or a psychopath. It's going to take me a while to trust she won't wake up and leave me again.

CHAPTER SEVEN

FAITH

N olan's heart beats beneath my cheek in a strong, steady rhythm—unlike the galloping pace of my own. My mind is finding it difficult to keep up, too.

From Nolan tossing me over his shoulder at church to spanking me in this small clearing, this may be the wildest Sunday of my life.

"What were you doing at my church this morning?" The question has swirled around in my head from the moment I laid eyes on his commanding form marching down the sanctuary aisle toward me.

"Some of your congregants have been harassing the club. Showing up unannounced at the compound to spout about our future in hell. Leaving pamphlets about the sins we're committing in our mailbox. Our club president, Snow, thought we could broker a peace with your dad by going to church like good folks. Guess I fucked that up."

"I had no idea those things were happening!" I lean back in his embrace to make sure he sees the truth in my gaze. "Dad speaks about the Reaper's Wolves sometimes, but I didn't realize those sermons had progressed to harassment. I'm so sorry."

"It's not your fault." He caresses my cheek before tucking a strand of hair behind my ear. "Where's your mom in all of this? Is she like your dad?"

"No, she died when I was three. I barely remember her. It's just me and Dad... and our church community."

Which really isn't much of a community for me. Most of our attendees are older. The only person younger than me is Mercy Campion, and her uncle keeps a tight leash on his only niece.

I rarely get to speak with Mercy anymore. She's always sequestered in a back pew with Lonny.

"And they're all like your dad?" Nolan guesses, stroking his thumb down my arm. I love the feeling of security his touch gives me. I want to stay tucked away with him, but I know that's not realistic.

Even if Nolan considers me "his woman"—a fact I'm still trying to wrap my head around—there's no way my father would ever approve of our relationship.

I'd like to say it doesn't matter, but he's my only family. Owns the home I live in. Is the reason I have a job at the church, though it doesn't pay enough for me to move out of the house. If I go against his wishes, I'll be kicked out and destitute.

Nolan seems like a good guy, but I don't expect him to take on the responsibility of an extra person.

"Yeah... It's pretty much been me and the old librarian Ms. Haversham as far as friends." And god, how sad that sounds.

"The librarian, huh?"

"You can thank her for even being open to sleeping with a man who isn't my husband."

"Really?"

Nodding, a teasing grin spreads. "Yeah, she introduced an entire new world to me through romance novels." I jab a finger into his chest. "And before you scoff or laugh, don't."

"It never crossed my mind, though I'm curious about these novels. Tell me more about those." He nuzzles into my hair before kissing the top of my ear.

Blushing, I shake my head in refusal, especially since I've been obsessed with stories featuring tattooed biker hotties like Alaska. "They're not important—"

"I beg to differ. They're the difference between me never knowing the hot clasp of your pussy and understanding exactly how tight and wet you are for me. So, it's time to fess up or my palm might start twitching to spank it out of you."

I fidget on his lap at the sexy threat. Intimate spankings aren't like anything I imagined. When I read those scenes in books, I couldn't quite grasp the concept of how something meant for pain could be pleasurable. Until now. Until I felt the warmth of Nolan's palm lightly smack my bottom.

"What's it gonna be, princess? You gonna tell me or am I spanking that sweet ass of yours again?"

As tempting as it sounds to test him, I mumble the answer under my breath.

Mouth quirked to the side in amusement, he says, "MC romance, huh? I assume I'm the reason for the sudden interest? Or have you always been a fan?" A note of jealousy enters his voice at the end.

I roll my eyes. "You know very well you are the reason. Usually, I go for cowboys."

"Cowboys? I suppose I could be a cowboy of the sea. I've been fishing up north for the past six months. Catching wild sea bass. Does that count?"

"Not really." I giggle, enjoying the lighthearted banter. It's a marked contrast from the heavy cloud that's been hanging over my head since meeting Nolan. "But you get a pass because you have other admirable qualities."

"Do I?" His lips dip lower to my neck before biting down on the spot where he left a mark our first night together. "Be sure to share those with your dear old dad, why don't ya?"

The reminder of what's waiting for me at home sobers me. "Nolan, what are we doing? My dad is never going to accept you."

"And that's important to you?" he asks. "I don't mean for that to be a shitty question, but... Like I said, my dad's a bastard, too, and I don't give two fucks if he approves of me."

"My dad is my only family. He's all I have left. Call it guilt or love, but I don't think I'm ready to cut him out of my life." Not that I *can,* but I keep that part to myself.

I really should've stopped being a *good girl* years ago before it decided to bite me in the butt like now. Then I may not be nearing thirty without much to my name that isn't controlled by my dad.

Before Nolan can respond, sirens wail in the distance, drawing near until I see the blue and red lights flash through the trees.

"I'm guessing that's your dad arriving with the cavalry."

"I'm so sorry. I don't want you to go to jail or anything. I'll tell them this is all a big misunderstanding."

"You don't need to worry about anything, princess. I'll handle them. This isn't the club's first run-in with the law." He winks. I don't understand how he can be so cavalier about the police arriving to most likely arrest him for whatever ridiculous charge my father created.

Nolan helps me off the bike, drags my tights back up, then grabs my hand and leads me out of the clearing, following the wide trail we rode in on, until we're visible to the slew of cop cars and motorcycles at the front of the main clubhouse.

"Get your dirty hands off my daughter!" Dad shouts from behind Sheriff Carson. The sheriff turns to say something to my dad to calm him down, but he should know better than telling my dad to do anything he doesn't want to.

"What seems to be the problem, officer?" Nolan addresses the deputy on his right as the crowd parts to let us through.

"The problem is you kidnapped my daughter."

God, will he ever stop?

When Nolan shared the news about church members harassing the Reaper's Wolves members, I was shocked and embarrassed. A sick knot in my stomach told me it wasn't a far cry from what I would expect from them.

"Now, Reverend, let's keep it civil." Another deputy raises both of his hands in a calming gesture, and my dad fumes, smoke practically billowing from the top of his head. "Ma'am, is it true this man took you against your will from church this morning?"

"N...n...no," I stutter, the authoritative line of officers intimidating me.

"Don't lie, Faith Anne."

Nolan's hand squeezes mine, and I feel a little stronger with him at my side. "No, he didn't," I say more firmly a second time.

"You can see the lady is fine, and there's no need for all this fuss," Nolan adds. "It was a simple squabble between a consenting couple of adults."

Oh, no.

"Are you saying that you knew my daughter before today?" Dad questions, turning his glare towards me, but Nolan ignores him in favor of speaking with the deputy again.

"Are we good to go now?"

"Settle down, son. We have more questions. Why didn't you listen when the Reverend asked you to stop hauling his daughter out of the service? It's unusual to see a man—a stranger, no less—toss a God-fearing woman like Miss Harris over his shoulder and take off. How do we know you haven't coerced her into something?"

The officer turns to me with kind eyes. "Ma'am, are you afraid? Is he threatening you in any way if you tell the truth?"

Oh my gosh, can this get any worse?

"No, officer, I promise I'm here of my own volition. Nolan's been a complete gentleman." If we ignore him stealing me away from church like a caveman and making me orgasm on his bike with just his fingers.

"Nolan?" A couple of club members question my use of his first name, and I wonder if I committed a motorcycle club faux pas. If I'm only supposed to call him Nolan when we're in private, and Alaska around everyone else.

"If that's true, then why don't you go on home with your daddy, Ms. Harris? You and Mr. Nolan here can work out your problems at a more civilized time when he's not interrupting your father's sermon."

"Like hell," Nolan growls, but the officer has a point. If I don't leave with my dad, who knows what he or the cops will do? I don't want to see anyone in cuffs on account of me. I'm already feeling like too much of a burden. Why would Nolan want me after all this trouble when he could have any of the women currently spilling out of the clubhouse? Women free to be with him without repercussions?

"It's okay. I'll go with Dad, and everything will be fine."

"No, I'm not losing you again."

"You're not. You know where I am. We'll see each other soon." *Maybe.* I'm not sure if we *will* cross paths again. Not because I don't want to, but because he might change his mind. Or fear might finally get the best of me again, and I stay away in order to keep my dad satisfied.

"Faith." Nolan stares me down as if he knows the direction of my thoughts, but I can be just as stubborn, especially when it comes to those I care about. And I really care about this big, protective biker, despite only knowing him for a short time.

"It'll be fine. Trust me." I squeeze his hand one last time before letting go, heading straight towards my father with my head held high. Ending the show that has everyone's attention riveted to the two of us.

The drive home is silent, Dad's anger building in the tense air between us. As soon as we're inside the house, it's like a match is lit because the explosion is immediate.

"What were you thinking, Faith? Hanging out with a man like that? How have you even met before today?"

I don't know how to answer his questions. I can't blame my trip to Seattle. Really, I can't mention any place for fear that he'll tell me to stay away from it, forbid me from going. "We ran into each other at the gas station," I lie.

'What did you say to him?"

"Nothing much. I was just polite."

Dad sighs, shaking his head in disappointment. "I know you don't have much experience with men, but you give guys like these an inch and they'll take a mile. The man stormed into my church service and stole you right from under my nose. Who knows what else he's done in his life or what he's planning next?"

"He's not dangerous. Aren't the Reaper's Wolves all former military men? I thought we were supposed to support our veterans," I say, playing the patriotic card.

"We don't know what those men's services looked like. Of course, we support our troops. But most don't come home and cause trouble like their group."

"What trouble? Aren't we the ones being a nuisance?"

"What's that supposed to mean?"

My mouth zips shut under his harsh gaze. Ducking my head, I mumble, "I heard that members of our church have been showing up unannounced at their compound. Harassing them."

"Is that what he's been telling you? Those lies?"

"Are they lies?" *Shut up! Stop pushing him!*

"You trust him over your own father?" His disbelief is obvious. I've never been one to argue with him, and now I'm choosing a biker's word over his own.

"I'm just looking for facts," I placate.

"The *facts*," he spits,"are you are my daughter, and I forbid you from seeing that man or any of his friends again. Do you understand me?"

"Dad, I'm an adult. I'm twenty-eight years old."

"You're a young, single woman who lives under my roof, and I don't condone the kind of behavior they allow at their clubhouse. If that's the kind of life you want, then I'm not sure what went wrong. Because I didn't teach you to behave that way."

"Behave what way? I haven't done anything wrong."

"You willingly left with that man and then defended him when the sheriff and I went to save you. You didn't protest once as he snatched you out of the church. Almost like you wanted to go with him." My dad's suspicious tone worries me. If he thinks for a second that Nolan and I are together, I'll be out of the house quicker than one of the little old ladies at church can say *bless her heart*.

"I was shell-shocked." That, at least, is the truth.

"Be sure that's all it was," Dad harrumphs and stalks past me, issuing a final warning to stay away from Nolan before leaving to smooth things over at the church after this morning's interruption.

With him gone, I sink into a kitchen chair and slump forward, staring unseeing out the window where a bird is resting on a swinging branch. Oh, to be a red-winged cardinal. Free to fly away. Unencumbered my familial expectations.

Able to be with whoever I choose without repercussions.

"FAITH, COME TO MY STUDY," Dad calls for me from the doorway of the kitchen where I'm preparing our Tuesday dinner. This is the first time he's talked to me since Sunday after lecturing me about Nolan.

Wiping my hands on a dish towel, I follow him down the hall to his study where Beau Adams sits in front of my dad's desk. I didn't even realize we had a guest.

"Take a seat next to Beau." Dad gestures to the second empty leather chair before relaxing behind the desk, steepling his fingers on the wooden top as he leans forward. "I've been thinking about your actions lately, and how it's partially my fault for your wild antics."

"What do you mean?" It's the first time my dad has taken responsibility for anything, so this is definitely a surprise.

"You're a twenty-eight-year-old woman past her prime. You should be married with a couple of children hanging onto your skirts by now. I've been lax in allowing you the freedom to choose your future husband. That was a mistake I'll be rectifying immediately."

Rectifying? Nervous sweat dampens my forehead. Usually, the women in our church marry young, and Dad preaches about having as many kids as possible to honor the Lord. How that's a woman's most vital duty.

Frankly, I've been thankful to slip under his radar this long. He's never tried to push me towards anyone, and though I've wondered why, I was never going to mention it and bring attention to the oversight.

"It's obvious you've never had any intention of marrying one of the good men of our church, and with your plain looks and gluttonous body, despite the stature of being my daughter, none of the men have come forward to ask for your hand. Until now, that is."

His insults prick my skin. So, that's why he never pushed anybody on me. No one was interested, and he felt bad for the guys, not for me.

Glancing between him and Beau, who's been sitting quietly the entire time, the puzzle pieces fall into place. "I'm not marrying Beau."

"It's not up to you—" Dad's voice begins to rise as his cheeks turn a ruddy color.

"Now, now, let's not get hostile," Beau interrupts. "Faith isn't being unreasonable with her concerns about marrying me. We talked about this, reverend. Faith isn't used to attention from a man, which is why it was so easy for that biker to get his claws in her. But we're fixing that now. Faith and I will court, and she'll see how she should be treated." He finishes his diatribe proudly—my father's obvious sycophant.

I hate that they're talking about me as if I'm not here, as if I'm a child, a sixteen-year-old girl going out on her first date. I'm not some naive little virgin. Not anymore.

Words crowd my throat. I want to shout into the room, but I remain quiet like I always do.

Stupid, cowardly, *silent* mouse.

"Son, I appreciate what you're wanting to do here, and I've agreed to a short courtship to make things look respectable, but Faith needs to learn not to talk back to her elders."

"When are Beau and I supposed to start courting?" I ask, my mind racing to figure out how to escape this arrangement.

"Tomorrow. He'll be taking you to the Wednesday small group he leads."

Our first date, if you could call it that, is going to be his small group? I almost laugh at the absurdity. This may be the most *Christian-ese* thing I've ever experienced.

"And how long will this courtship last before we're expected to marry?"

"One month, then we'll announce the engagement. Everyone will understand the haste, considering your age, and this recent trouble."

One month, and then they expect me to be Mrs. Beau Adams.

Not in this lifetime.

CHAPTER EIGHT

ALASKA

The ragged punching bag explodes from the force of my fist ramming into its center. Held up by duct tape and jagged stitching, it's a miracle it withstood my punches for so long. Grim's dog, Tiny, barks in annoyance, shaking off the dusting of cloth and sand.

"Sorry, bud." I pat his blockhead apologetically. The club bought an old gym to fix up for a new business on High Ridge's Main Street, and this shitty punching bag would have been trashed eventually. Guess I just hurried it along.

"Still upset about Sunday?" Grim asks from his position on the floor, ripping up the rotted hardwood.

"Wouldn't you be? I had to let my girl walk off without a word. That's the second time she's left me." Kicking the fallen punching bag with my foot, I grunt in pain at the impact of my toes on the solid center.

"And that's two times too many? What happens if she gets a third strike? She's not your girl anymore?"

"Shut your fucking mouth. Of course not. She gets as many strikes as she needs." My feelings will never change, no matter what she does, but it's frustrating as fuck.

"What are you gonna do? It's not like a preacher's daughter is gonna turn against her daddy for you." Grim smirks as he looks me up and down.

Yeah, I know I'm a giant motherfucker covered in tattoos and a beard—my leather cut announcing to the world my membership in the Reaper's Wolves MC. I'm a former army sniper with kills under my belt. What normal father would want that for his daughter? And Faith's dad? He's as far from normal as you can get, so I know my cause is hopeless. But I'm not going to let that stop me.

Because Faith is mine.

And she's suffocating in that toxic environment.

"I don't know yet. I'd say it's her move, but I feel like her dad keeps her locked up pretty tight."

"So, it's gonna be you who breaks her out?"

"Damn straight." Now that I know her dad's the preacher of that church, I also know her address. Little recon should let me know which room is hers and how to get in without detection.

My mind runs through the possibilities until a familiar form casts a shadow from the glass front windows of the gym, and I grit my teeth at the sight.

"You've got to be fucking kidding me."

"What?" Grim looks up and sees the cause of my annoyance—Snake, my no-account dad. "He's got a lot of nerve showing his face around here. Even if he is your old man. How'd he know where to find you?"

"Hell if I know, but I'll deal with him." Wiping the sweat off my face with the bottom of my shirt, I take a moment to prepare myself before confronting Snake.

He's more his former club name than "Dad" to me anyway. Reptilian. Slick.

An autumn breeze ruffles my hair as I step outside. "What the hell are you doing here?"

"Heard you were back in town and causing a ruckus with the preacher's daughter." Snake snickers. "Didn't peg you to go for the virtuous type."

"Don't presume to know anything about me. Snow's dad was more a father to me than you ever were. The club raised me, not you, And how did you repay them? By stealing their shit and fucking around with another club."

"I see how well the club raised you," Snake sneers, spitting a piece of tobacco onto the sidewalk.

Disgusting.

"You treat your old man like I'm a piece of shit stuck to your boot. After I tried to get a better life for you and the rest of those choir boys. We deserve more than the measly allowance Snow doles out. The Ghost Riders understand that."

"The Ghost Riders are a bunch of criminal dipshits if they thought tying up with you was a good idea. Didn't you get enough time behind bars after your DWI?"

He shakes his head in disappointment, ignoring my dig about his past arrests. Dear old dad was no stranger to breaking the law and spending time in jail. "They've brainwashed you, boy."

Like I give a shit how he feels about me.

"But that's why I'm here. To try and talk some sense into you. There's a job coming up. A big one and..."

I raise my hands to stop him. "And I don't wanna hear about it. You wanna fuck up your life? Have at it. But you're not screwing with mine."

"Trust me, you're gonna want in on this. A little extra money may even land you the preacher's daughter. Give some to her daddy's church."

A snarl of warning curls my lips. "Don't mention Faith again. Don't come around anymore. I'm already trying to patch things up with the club after your stunt. I don't need you trying to rope me into another one of your schemes."

Snake cracks his knuckles. "Stubborn son of a bitch. Just like your old man."

"I'm nothing like you."

"Keep telling yourself that." He retreats to a beat up old hog and gives a two-finger wave. "Think about what I said. I'll see around, son."

That's exactly what I'm afraid of.

"WHAT'S GOING ON?" APPREHENSION tightens my shoulders as I enter the tech room to see Snow, Fox, and Ollie waiting for me. It's been twenty-four hours since the altercation with my dad, and I was just starting to relax when Snow sent me a text asking me to join them for some important club business.

"Show him," Snow says, and Ollie pulls up security footage on his multiple screens. A grainy black and white video begins to play. Snake is holding a gas station clerk at gunpoint as they empty the cash register—his Reaper's Wolves cut clearly visible.

"Fuck, how'd he get his cut back? We stripped that of him when he was kicked out of the club." Fox must be seeing this for the first time, too.

Snake didn't like that the club conducted their business legally through a couple of strip clubs, an auto body shop, and soon the renovated gym Grim and I were working on. They made a profit without requiring us to use them for illegal business as well—not that we ever would. Plus, with the brains of Dex, our treasurer, we invested most of our profits to build an even nicer nest egg.

Somehow that wasn't enough for my dad, though.

He thinks running drugs and weapons is where we should earn our money.

"He must've snuck it out somehow. Or made one himself?" Ollie offers an explanation.

"However, he did it, he needs to be stopped. He's stirring up too much trouble and painting a target on our backs. The cops in High Ridge and Everton have already been giving us shit. We don't need an ex-member causing more problems." Snow crosses his arms and stares at me. "Grim mentioned that Snake stopped by to see you yesterday. What did he want?"

Damn, I knew his visit was going to bite me in the ass. *Fucking Grim.* "The usual. Wants me to join him for some deal. I don't know what it is, and I don't want to know."

"Maybe you should find out, so we know what the hell is going on in that fucked-up mind of his. Where is he now, Ollie?"

"According to this security footage, his last known location was Buskin Falls, a six hour ride from here. Then a couple of stoplight cameras picked him up. It looks like he's headed towards Tallulah." Ollie points to red marks on a map that take a northeastern route.

"Demons territory? Why the hell is he headed there?"

The Shadow Demons MC is the epicenter for every scumbag and tweaker on this side of the Mississippi. They don't follow any rules, and their president is batshit crazy. Makes the run-in we had with the Ghost Riders MC look downright civilized based on the reports I've heard about our dealings with the club.

"Keep tracking his movements and see if we can find out what he's up to. We don't need another club thinking to steal what's ours." Snow turns to me. "If he contacts you, tell me. I don't want to hear it through the grapevine again. Got it? You're already on thin ice after the Sunday stunt."

"Understood. You'll be the first to hear of any news, Prez."

He dismisses us, and I escape outside as my mind struggles to figure out Snake's next move. He's never been the smartest member of the club, but what he lacks in smarts, he makes up for in sheer guts.

My dad's never shied away from a dangerous mission and dives headfirst into risky situations before assessing the consequences.

Whatever he has planned now is sure to wreak havoc on our lives if I don't find a way to stop him.

CHAPTER NINE

FAITH

Wednesday morning I walk into the library and immediately find Ms. Haversham at the front counter checking in a stack of books. As soon as she sees me, her eyes widen behind her square-framed glasses, and she makes a clucking sound with her tongue.

"Girl, what have you done? Everybody's talking about the drama at church Sunday."

I groan, dropping my head into my hands as I wilt against the counter. It's just us this morning since our tiny library isn't the most popular place in town. "The morning started off normal," I begin, then relay Nolan's arrival and subsequent kidnapping of me. The only part I leave out is what happened between us on his motorcycle at the compound. I'm sure Ms. Haversham would love to hear about my escapade, but those are private details between me and him.

Ms. Haversham fans herself. "Oh, hun, what I wouldn't give to be in your shoes."

"What?" I ask incredulously.

"You know, minus your father." She rolls her eyes. Ms. Haversham and my dad went to school together, so she's known him longer than I've even been alive. Apparently, he's always maintained a holier-than-thou personality that rubbed her the wrong way.

"I like how you're subtracting Dad but leaving a real-life motorcycle club member. Club's just a euphemism for gang, right?" I'm teasing, and Ms. Haversham takes me seriously.

She shakes her head. "Not with these guys. They're military veterans. It's more about brotherhood than what you've seen on TV with *Sons of Anarchy.*"

"You know I've never seen that show…"

"But you've seen Jax Teller," she says with a pointed stare. I hem and haw with a smile because she knows me too well.

"What are you going to do next?" she asks, lowering her voice as an older gentleman enters the library, heading straight for the historical fiction section.

"I don't know. Nolan said I'm *his,*" my voice drops to imitate his gravelly tone. "He didn't act like he was just going to disappear, but Dad… His thoughts on the Reaper's Wolves are obvious, and now I have Beau to contend with."

"No, you don't. There's no way you're marrying that boy. I've known him since he was in diapers, just like you. He can be sweet when he wants to be, but he's not the man for you."

"Dad thinks he is, and he's all that matters."

"Yeah, when your dad gets a thought in his head, he can be pretty stubborn." A worried look crosses her face.

"I know. If I don't agree to marry Beau, I might be out on the street," I voice the fear I've been harboring ever since things started spiraling Sunday.

"You always have a home with me. I've been telling you for years you need to move out of that house."

"I know, I know." She's been wanting me to venture out on my own ever since I graduated high school. But I knew the moment I moved out by myself, my dad would take issue with it because I'm an unmarried woman.

He's very conservative and old-fashioned in his beliefs. Single daughters stay with their parents until they marry. Since my job is dependent on him at the church, I didn't want to make waves.

However, it might be time since Nolan crashed into my life like a freaking tsunami.

"I don't want to put you out," I hedge.

The older gentleman steps up behind me with a book in hand, and I quickly excuse myself, promising to call Ms. Haversham later tonight if I have any updates. When I'm back in my car, I contemplate what to do with the rest of my day. Dad gave me the day off from helping at the church in order to prepare for my date with Beau tonight at small group. He warned me to think about my future.

I played it off with Ms. Haversham, but it really is an ultimatum. *Marry Beau or get out.* I just don't know where to *get out* to. I don't want to inconvenience Ms. Haversham. She lives in a tiny apartment with her two little dachshunds. There's not really room for a second person.

Besides, my problems aren't hers, no matter how kind she is.

I turn the key in the ignition and pull out of the library parking lot, mindlessly driving until the welcome sign for Suitor's Crossing greets me thirty-minutes later. Their Main Street is a sweet storefront-lined lane with cute shops and boutiques. High Ridge has a similar thoroughfare, but ours is a little older and not as well kept.

Probably because we don't get as many tourists. Everyone prefers visiting a town linked to a romantic legend of soulmates, and I don't blame them.

The scent of coffee floats in the air, and the comforting aroma lures me into Brewed, the local coffee shop. Maybe caffeine will kick start ideas about my future.

Or fate will play its hand... Because once I'm inside, I recognize the girl who was with the Reaper's Wolves on Sunday at a corner table sitting across from another woman with their laptops and coffees.

"Hey!" She waves me over with a smile after I pick up my iced mocha. "Faith, right? I'm Caroline, and this is my friend Lindy."

"Nice to meet you," I say gingerly, lowering into an empty seat at their table.

"You're kind of a ways from home, aren't you?"

"Yeah, I thought I'd get out of town for a little bit."

"I get it. Is your dad still pissed about Alaska?" Empathy fills her eyes, and a sense of calm settles over my shoulders at her non-judgmental tone.

I nod and glance down, tracing the condensation around my cup.

"Obviously, I don't know you very well, or your dad, so take this with a grain of salt. Tell me to shut up, and I will. But he doesn't seem very open to building a peace between the Reaper's Wolves MC and your church. The phone's been ringing off the hook this morning at our auto body shop, since they know we own it."

"Are you serious?" I ask, ashamed to hear the news.

"What happened with Alaska pushed everything over the edge. Caused tensions to rise even higher. Alaska got a stern talking to from my husband because of it."

"Oh, you're married?"

She smiles. "Recently, yes. My husband is Logan Snow. He's the president of the Reaper's Wolves MC."

"Wow." I can feel the shock on my face because she's not who I would typically view as a biker's wife. Even though I knew she was associated with them.

"Surprising, isn't it?" Lindy smirks. They share a look before turning back to me. "But trust me, they're good guys."

Caroline nods and reaches over to clasp my hand. "I don't really know what's going on between you and Alaska, aside from the fact he's clearly taken with you, but if you have any misgivings with the fact that he's part of an MC, don't. I already went through that with Logan, so I'll save you the trouble. They're totally legit, not into anything sketchy. You don't have to worry about getting into something you're not ready for as far as the law and that kind of stuff goes." She laughs. "Relationship-wise... It could be a roller coaster. But I'm happy with Logan."

"You ought to be." Lindy jokes. "You should see the two of them."

"I'd like that. I'm not sure what's going to happen with Alaska, but he's kind of the least of my worries right now," I admit, reverting back to Nolan's club name with the women.

"Oh? Feel free to share." Caroline offers a kind smile. "We promise it'll be just between us girls. Plus, sometimes it's good to get an outsider's point of view or advice."

I'm not sure what they could possibly say to help me with this situation, but I can't resist the opportunity of sharing with girlfriends. It's an experience I've never really had before except with Ms. Haversham, and she's at least thirty years older than me.

"My dad hates the Reaper's Wolves, and he's really conservative. Technically, by our church's unofficial rules, I should have been married long ago and have a passel of children. But I don't. I'm still single." I sigh. "Dad isn't going to let that fly anymore after the debacle with Alaska. It's either marry an associate pastor at our church or leave the house because I'm not following his rules."

"Are you serious?"

"Unfortunately, yes. It's pathetic really that I even put myself in this position. No home. Potentially no job because my dad arranged for my position at the church to keep me close. I don't really have a lot of savings because I don't need much since I live with him. I've kind of screwed myself over."

Unexpected tears well up as I consider my situation. I've always known in the back of my mind that if anything terrible truly happened to me, I would be in trouble. But I always dismissed the fear because what could happen to me?

I've lived twenty-eight years following my dad's rules, however reluctantly at times, and it suited me fine when I was able to read and work and keep to myself. But then Nolan came into my life, and now I have to make these decisions and force my dad's hand.

It scares me because if I lose him, I lose my family.

Both my parents were only children. My grandparents have long passed. It would just be me left. And as much as I hate living with my dad and being under his thumb, at least he's someone who cares for me. As tenuous as it seems.

At least I know how to handle living with him.

He's the known versus the unknown of everything outside our bubble.

"I'm so sorry he's doing that to you," Lindy says, reaching across the table to pat my hand in comfort.

I blink away the tears and force a smile that probably resembled more of a grimace. "Thanks. I'll figure it out. I didn't mean to burden you with my problems."

"No, you totally did the right thing by sharing. I was in a similar situation. Not with my dad, but with an ex-boyfriend. Caroline and the Reaper's Wolves really helped me out, and I think this is my time to pay it forward." She glances at Caroline, who's tapping away on her phone and nods in whatever agreement they're silently coming to. "Why don't you come stay with me on the compound?"

"What? I couldn't—"

"Hear me out. Logan lets me rent a cabin for a reasonable price on the property. It's totally safe. The guys won't bother you. There's enough room for another person because there's a guest room and an office. We can help you get back on your feet."

"I couldn't ask that of you. You barely know me."

"We know enough. We like you. Alaska likes you. And if he finds out what's going to happen, I have no doubt he'll lock you away in his room at the clubhouse." Lindy must read my wariness. "Don't get me wrong, you might enjoy it, but it can get a little rowdy there with all the guys partying."

"Yeah, that doesn't really sound like my scene." Even if staying in Alaska's bed does get me hot and bothered.

You should not be thinking about sex right now.

You're having a major life crisis.

"Think about it. You don't have to say yes right now," Lindy says. "But I get the impression this is an urgent matter. That your dad's not exactly the patient type. So just say the word, and you've got a room with me. We can help figure out a job for you, too, I'm sure."

This time I can't stop the tears from falling as I self-consciously swipe at them with my fingers, a small, embarrassed chuckle escaping. "I don't know what to say. I should say no, but I feel like maybe..."

"You should say yes." Lindy stands up and immediately bends down to hug me in my seat.

"You should. It's decided." Caroline agrees. "Logan's cool with it. Which, if he hadn't been, he would have gotten cool with it real fast. Trust me." She winks. "Just let us know if you need help moving or packing or anything, and we'll come."

"Really? Just like that?" I ask.

"Just like that. It's what happened to me, too. Don't worry. They're kind of used to this by now."

Releasing a heavy breath, I suddenly feel drained, despite the morning hour. "Thank you."

"You are very welcome."

After coordinating with Lindy and Caroline, we decide to jump feet first into the move and schedule to meet up the next morning to set things in motion. I even managed to avoid my date with Beau last night by claiming my period started and wasn't feeling well. Dad wasn't too happy, but he couldn't exactly question biology.

God's handiwork and all.

Dust kicks up on the long dirt drive as a blue truck and an SUV drive toward the house.

"Who can that be?" Dad asks from his spot in the living room watching a show about the Roman Empire.

I didn't warn him about my plans today, wanting to head off any trouble like him deciding to kick me out immediately. But now that the cavalry had arrived, it's time to drop the news.

"I'm moving out."

"Excuse me?"

"You want me to marry Beau, and I can't. I don't love him." Glancing between him and outside to track the progress of vehicles coming our way, I ask, "Can you honestly say if I don't marry Beau, you won't kick me out for disobeying you? Isn't that what you told the Pearsons to do with Joanie back when I was ten?"

I'd forgotten about the incident until recently. Now that it resembles my own life. Because Joanie chose not to marry Deacon Morris.

"I would hope we'd avoid any need for you to leave because you'd want to do as I tell you," he grits out, trying to hang on to his composure. "Love can grow, Faith. It's your duty to obey me as your father."

Inching toward the front door, my trembling hands unlock the door and turn the knob. "I don't think God would approve of me marrying someone I don't love. It's high time I move out on my own and start taking care of myself."

"That's not what we do. Where do you expect to go? You don't have any savings, and you won't have a job if you move out. I'm not supporting a disrespectful daughter."

A door slams outside, and he glares out the window. I follow his gaze to see Caroline and Lindy, along with a couple of men in leather cuts, showcasing their Reaper's Wolves affiliation. One man is very recognizable as Alaska as he marches up the steps to the porch. I swing the door open to let them in.

"This is your plan, hmm? You're going to go live with that man and sin?"

"No, Dad. I'm going to stay with Lindy. She's a friend."

"Who's also a *friend* of these heathens. I knew there was something more between you and that man. Now you're proving it."

Ignoring him, I greet the group here to help. "Hey, my room is upstairs to the right, if you just want to grab things." I tried to pack what I could discreetly.

"Don't come into my house!" Dad shouts.

"This is my home, too. They can go to my room."

"You used to live here," Dad corrects me. "Anything under this roof is mine. You can leave with the clothes on your back."

"Are you fucking kidding me?" Alaska asks, stepping in front of me. "She'll take whatever she goddamn pleases."

Caroline, Lindy, and two other men head upstairs with purpose.

"Don't swear at me, young man. I'll have the sheriff back out here to arrest all of you for trespassing."

"Dad, relax. This is what you wanted, right? You gave me a choice, even if it was unspoken. Beau or move out. I choose the latter."

"Who the fuck is Beau?" Alaska growls, his gaze ping-ponging between me and Dad. He's standing next to me, his hand on the small of my back, heated frustration wafting from him.

"He's no one," I say, allowing myself to relax a little into his side.

"No one? Is that how you describe a man of God who's been like family for years? How quickly they've corrupted you."

"The only corrupt influence around here is you." Alaska jabs my dad's chest with his finger. Probably not the best decision.

"Touch me again. Do you want to add assault to trespassing?"

"Fear tactics might work with your congregation, but you don't scare me, reverend."

"Alaska, I've got this," I murmur, using his road name rather than his first name since it seems too intimate in front of my father.

"I'm not leaving you alone with him."

"Don't pretend to be chivalrous." Dad barks. "Are you so easily fooled?" He jerks his thumb toward Alaska. "A man says some pretty words to you, and you fall at his feet. I'm ashamed to have you as a daughter."

That one hurts like a punch to the gut. "You should be ashamed of yourself, Dad. You haven't treated me kindly since Mom died, and I don't know what I did to deserve your ire."

I don't wait for a response. Instead, I head upstairs with Alaska following my steps. Within an hour, we'd packed the two trucks with my belongings, my bed, my dresser, and my mom's old hope chest.

It's been quiet downstairs, and I figured Dad might have left to avoid being in these *heathens'* presence, but he must have just been working himself into a lather. Because right as we're exiting the house, he grabs my arm and yanks me back.

I wince, a sound of pain falling from my lips as he shakes my arm. "You're going to regret this, Faith. And when you do, don't come crying back to me because you won't be welcome. You lie with dogs, you get fleas." He tosses my arm away like it disgusts him, and Alaska's right there, shoving him against the front door.

"You ever touch her again, and I will fucking bury you. Understand?" Dad's face is purple as he gasps for air. He doesn't respond, but Alaska lets him go with a curse, ushering me down the steps and helping me into the second truck.

"Are you alright?"

"Yeah, I'm fine." Rubbing my arm, I stare out at the place that's been home for almost three decades. It's seen better days. The yellow paint used to be brighter. The stone steps weren't cracked. I've tried keeping it in good shape, but there's only so much a person could do in the face of time and weather.

Nolan climbs into the driver's seat and starts the truck.

"You're driving? What about your bike?" Logically, I realize he can't ride it everywhere, but it's still unexpected to see him behind a wheel rather than handlebars.

"Left it at the compound." He makes a left at the end of the drive, following Caroline and Lindy in the truck ahead while the men who helped escort us on their bikes.

The cabin remains quiet until Nolan sighs and reaches across the console to rest a hand on my thigh. "I'm sorry about your dad. He never should've forced you to choose marriage or a home. That's fucking barbaric."

Resting my head on the window, I agree, welcoming the comforting warmth of his palm radiating through my jeans to encompass my entire body. "It's the way of our church. Men hold all the power. Husbands. Fathers. The fact that my dad is also lead pastor makes it even worse. He's got double the authority."

"And abuses it."

"Unfortunately." Red and orange leaves blend together in a fiery collage as we drive down the interstate toward Suitor's Crossing. Soon everything will be bare, ready for winter snow. "It's my fault for things getting this bad, though. If I'd left after high school... Or found a different job, one not reliant on him..."

"Don't blame yourself for his shortcomings. He's your fucking father. A man who's supposed to love you unconditionally. Instead, he gave you little choice in your life and chose to punish you for the decisions you did make." Nolan's grip on the steering wheel tightens until his knuckles turn white. "Trust me. I know all about shitty dads. None of this is your fault."

That's the second time he's mentioned issues with his dad. Curious, I probe for more information, desperate to forget about my own father for a minute.

"What's wrong with your dad?"

A rumble of amusement comes from his chest. "Baby, I could fill an entire road trip from here to Florida with what's wrong with Snake. That's his road name. His most recent fuck-up was conspiring with another club to steal from our businesses in Everton. That's actually how Snow and Caroline met. Well, sort of."

"What?" He wasn't kidding. His dad does sound on par with mine. Who works against his MC, his son's MC, just for money? The club's supposed to be about loyalty, brotherhood. At least that's how the romance novels I read portray motorcycle clubs.

"Yep. Snake thinks we'd do better financially by stealing, running drugs and weapons, rather than working hard. Snow kicked him out of the club, but he's still causing trouble. He came to see me the other day."

Covering his hand with my own, I feel the rigidity in his grip and attempt to soothe him by tracing his fingers, one by one. They're thick with blunt fingernails, and unbidden, a memory of them plunging into my core flashes in my head.

Not the time!

"How'd you feel about his visit?"

"Annoyed," he huffs. "He acted like he didn't do anything wrong. That I was the one with a problem. Like no, motherfucker, you're the one who wronged the club and put me in the middle of it." His fist slammed into the wheel before gaining control again. "And he wants to drag me into another scheme, too."

"I'm so sorry. You deserve love and respect, not manipulation."

"So, do you, princess." He tips his head to meet my eyes for one intimate second then returns to watching the road. I study his profile—the rugged beard, longish chestnut hair, a slight bump in his nose—and marvel at my good fortune.

Sure, my dad practically disowned me, but I have Nolan. An understanding giant of a man who desires *me*. Five foot two, curves to spare, romance bookworm Faith Anne Harris.

I thread my fingers with his as we sit in companionable silence for the rest of the trip, hope blooming in my chest.

CHAPTER TEN

FAITH

A bell rings above my head as I enter Dusty's Auto Shop. Caroline managed to get me a receptionist job with the Reaper's Wolves local mechanic, and today is my first day. It's a cute shop, although a little run down. Old-fashioned decor, which probably was new when it was hung, reflects the sunlight—faded to gentle hues while dust motes float in the air.

"Are you Faith?" A guy comes out of the back, wiping his hands with a stained blue rag. He's a big man, like most of the Reaper's Wolves MC members, and I wonder if it's something in the Suitor's Crossing water supply that produces muscled giants.

"That's me."

"Wes. Snow said you'd be by this morning. This will be your setup." He waves toward the counter which has an updated computer at least. "I'll walk you through our software, but it's pretty simple. Snow said you're used to this kind of stuff?"

"Yes." I nod eagerly. "I assisted at my church in their office, so I should get the hang of it quickly."

"Great." He clicks around on the screen, walking me through each step of how to set up appointments, take payments, and how the phones work. All in all, it's a thirty-minute orientation, and I'm grateful for his straightforward manner.

"If you need anything else, just holler. Me and the guys will be in the back."

"Sounds good. Thank you so much for taking a chance on me. I really appreciate it."

"No problem. Snow vouched for you, so we're good." Wes disappears in the back, and I sit down at my new desk with a sigh of relief. Everything seems too good to be true. A reasonably priced room with Lindy. A good job. Friends that seem to multiply from Caroline to Lindy to Caroline's book club girls who I have yet to meet.

Don't forget Nolan.

How could I? It'd be easy to blame him for the trajectory my life has taken the past week or so, but I'm the one who wanted to break out of my bubble and go to Seattle in the first place. I was looking for a change, searching for myself. In the process, Nolan found me.

So, really, I set all of this in motion.

Who knew one short vacation would flip my entire world upside down?

CHAPTER ELEVEN

ALASKA

I pull up to Dusty's Auto Shop and cut the engine of my motorcycle. Faith's inside working, and I'm here to see my girl after dealing with my dad's shit this past week. He hasn't surfaced since Ollie's last update, staying uncharacteristically quiet. It makes the back of my neck itch like it used to in the service—a warning sign of things to come.

A chime rings overhead as I step inside the cool interior. Despite Faith living on the compound, we haven't seen each other much. But that's about to change.

"Hey, princess."

"Nolan, I wasn't expecting to see you today. Your name's not on our appointment book." She taps away on the computer, her button nose scrunching as she searches for my name on the screen, and looking ridiculously adorable as she does it in a green sweater that molds to her generous tits.

Fuck, I remember how sweet they tasted in my mouth.

It's been too long since I've had my teeth tugging at her nipples, my cock filling her pussy. A problem I'm ready to solve.

"That's because I'm just here to see you." I rest my crossed arms on the countertop and lean forward, staring down into her violet eyes. They're a shade that shouldn't be natural, but with her, it proves how unique her beauty is.

"Oh…" A pink blush rises from her neck to her cheeks, and I grin.

"I'm hoping you're done running from me, and we can have an official date."

"Running from you?"

I tick off the points with my fingers. "First the hotel, then last Sunday with your dad."

"Trust me, it's a good thing I left with him or else we would have had even more issues."

"Issues I can handle, princess. Losing you is not one of them. About that date… How's tonight? Dinner?"

Faith focuses on the computer monitor before peeking up at me through her lashes. Damn, she's cute. Demure. Hesitant. But beneath that shy exterior, there's a little wanton waiting to be unleashed. Again.

"Um, sure. I get off today at six."

"Why don't I pick you up from Lindy's cabin around seven? Give you time to do whatever you gotta do to get ready."

"That'll work. See you then."

"You can count on it." She smiles, and I wish I could drag her across the counter and kiss those cherry red lips, but I bide my time.

Soon enough we'll be together. I just have to be patient.

THE SOUND OF POWER tools fills the old gym space as Grim and Timber work on resanding the floor. Masks and safety glasses cover their faces, but they offer a wave in greeting while I grab my own gear to start helping them.

The physical labor is a much-needed outlet for the energy pent up inside me. I want to find Snake and shake some sense into him. What the hell is he thinking of robbing gas stations and mom and pop grocery stores? They don't hold the big pay day he's always looking to score.

Then there's Faith. She agreed to our date tonight, but I'm not sure where her head's at after the confrontation with her own bastard father.

What a pair we make. Two different people yet plagued by similar trouble from our shitty dads.

"Alaska!" My name's shouted over the din of whining machines, and I glance up to see Snow pointing toward the back office. Nodding in understanding, I wrap up what I'm doing before finding Snow seated behind a dusty desk that's tilted to the left.

"What's up?"

"Take a seat. I want to run something by you."

The rickety wooden chair groans beneath my weight, but thankfully, it holds. Damn, this entire building needs an overhaul—the previous owners didn't take care of shit.

"The gym's supposed to open the first of the new year, and we'll need a manager to run the day-to-day business. Is that something you'd be interested in?"

Can't fault Snow for beating around the bush. The man gets straight to the point.

"I'm not sure... Jessup's expecting me back up north in a couple of months." Jessup is the owner of the boat I work on while in Alaska. He's a grizzled old man, but he's been good to me. I'd hate to leave him in the lurch.

Snow angles his chin. "What about Faith? You're gonna leave her behind? I thought she was your woman."

"She is." I want her to be, but no matter how much I crave her, in the end, it's got to be Faith's decision to give us a fair shot. Maybe tonight I'll learn where we stand. "It's still early days. She needs time to figure out what she wants after dealing with her dad."

"Understandable. The man's a real piece of work. He still hasn't called off his hounds of righteous fury," Snow says, crumpling an old flier in his fist before tossing it at a wire trash can. Grunting when it misses. "You don't need to give me an answer about taking over the gym yet. We've got time. Let me know when you and Faith sort things out, okay?"

Nodding, I offer my hand and we shake on it.

Manager of the club's gym.

I've managed teams of men in the army, but this would be different. The club would be depending on me to run a profitable business. After exiting the office, I survey the gym space under a fresh light. Everything's in the middle of renovation now, but it's got potential.

The only dedicated gym area in Suitor's Crossing is at the YMCA, so I'm confident we'll have a steady flow of clients. Perhaps this is just what I need.

To settle in Suitor's Crossing.

Become a successful business manager.

Claim my woman for good.

A chance at stability and security Snake never offered me.

CHAPTER TWELVE

FAITH

"I hope this is okay," Alaska says as he helps me off his bike. The sun's already set, but cheerful golden lights sparkle across the porch circling The Ole Aces. Conversation filters through the doors, signaling a busy night for the bar and grill, despite it being Thursday.

"It's great. Lindy told me it's a popular hangout for the club since the owner Austin is best friends with Snow. I've been wanting to visit just to see if it's any different from No Man's Land."

The place is crowded with bikers and Suitor's Crossing citizens alike as we step inside. Groups sit at tables eating dinner while the bar is full of patrons. Nolan leads me to an open booth in a back corner, plucking the reserved sign off the table and folding it in half.

"You had them reserve a spot for us?" I ask, charmed by the notion of reserving anything in a place like this.

"Needed to ensure we had a private booth, considering how busy it gets." He waits for me to sit before sliding in next to me rather than across the table. The intimacy is surprising but not unwelcome.

"How's your week at the new job? Any problems?"

"Hardly. Wes was really helpful explaining things, and the customers are all friendly. To be honest, I actually like it better than working at the church." It didn't feel like I was under a microscope the entire room. Like if I made one wrong move—wasn't the perfect employee—then it'd reflect badly on my dad.

"Doesn't surprise me if you're used to working with people like your father or the ones harassing the club."

"I'm really sorry about that by the way. I brought it up to Dad, but he acted like it wasn't even happening."

"You don't need to apologize for him and his congregants. It's not your fault." Nolan drapes his arm across the back of the seat, warming my shoulders and neck, immediately distracting me. "I've had just enough about deadbeat dads this week."

"Because of your own?" I let my head rest on his arm, cozying up into his side. We're in a public place. It should embarrass me, being so forward, but Nolan's a draw I can't resist. He's been that way since we first met.

"Yeah..." He rubs the back of his neck and glances around the bar. "Has Lindy shared anything with you? Or Caroline?"

"Nope. All I know is what you've shared."

"It seems trying to rip off the club wasn't enough for him. He's taken to robbing a gas station and who knows what else while wearing a Reaper's Wolves MC cut. We've been searching for him, especially since it looks like he wants to team up with another club again."

"Oh, wow. Why is he obsessed with money?"

"He's always had dreams of living the high life of a biker. Thinks he's fucking Harry Bowman, but the club has never been about the shit Hell's Angels does. We've always been legit, just a home for returned military vets." Nolan's finger twists a strand of my hair into a corkscrew. His voice takes on a far-off quality. "That's what Snow's dad wanted. Snake was actually friends with him. They served together. Sometimes I wonder if Keys, Snow's dad, didn't just feel sorry for Snake, and that's why he patched him into the club. To set him on the straight and narrow."

"At least he tried, though I'm sorry he failed," I say, gingerly laying my hand over Nolan's heart. It's beating fast, and no wonder. Talking about his dad must rile him up.

"It's all good. The club raised me, and now I'm trying to live my own life."

Just like me now that I'm away from Dad.

Nolan picks up my hand and presses a kiss to the center of my palm before returning it to his chest. "Damn, look at me. I said we shouldn't talk about our dads anymore, and here I am ragging on about Snake," he groans.

A waitress stops by for our dinner order before hurrying off to another table. Her visit is like a reset button because Nolan straightens and peers down at me with determination flaring in his eyes.

"We've got more important things to discuss, don't we, princess?" The change in his tone raises the hair on the back of my neck and has me squeezing my thighs together. It's the same voice he used before making me come on his bike.

"We do?" I ask, playing dumb.

"The way I see it, you gave yourself to me the night we first met, but then you ran and then you left again last Sunday. I need to know what this is between us because I'm dead serious about you, princess."

Wow, he laid it out on the line in quick fashion. Blunt. Honest. Which means I need to be just as vulnerable.

"The night we spent together was the best night of my life. I finally felt free to be myself, but the next morning shame and guilt hit me hard."

"There's nothing to be ashamed about—"

I lift my hand to stop him. "Logically, I know that's true, but I've still grown up in a very conservative family. With very strict rules about virginity and only giving yourself to your husband in marriage. What we did was so far away from what I was taught to believe... Or even what I wanted for myself for the longest time."

"You regret it."

"No." My hand covers his where it's tapping a steady beat against the tabletop. His wrist twists to tangle his fingers around my smaller ones. "I don't regret it, but there *is* a small part of me that's grieving the dream I had."

Perhaps more than I realized now that I'm voicing it aloud.

"Despite reading all the romance novels and unlearning a lot of purity culture rules, I still imagined being in love with the man I had sex with for the first time. I imagined we would be in a serious relationship heading toward marriage, and none of that was true for us." Expelling a heavy breath, I finish, "I initiated things. I take full responsibility for my feelings, but it's a hard thing for me to wrap my head around."

Scooting over, I put some space between us, so I can face him more fully. He needs to know I'm serious about this next part. "Believe me when I say I'm trying. I want to see where things go between us."

Nolan studies me. There's an entire conversation bouncing between us. Unspoken in the air. Until finally, he nods, a slow grin peeking through his beard.

"Alright, that's what I needed to hear, princess."

CREDITS START TO ROLL as the movie ends, and Lindy stretches her arms above her head with a yawn. We're both comfy on separate couches, wrapped up in blankets, and it feels like what I assume living in a dorm with a roommate is like. I say as much to Lindy.

"You're right. This does bring me back to being in the dorm. We would stay up until two or three a.m. chatting. Lights out, in bed, not ready to fall asleep. Those were the days."

"I wish I'd gotten to experience those things. Sounds like perfect bonding moments." While girls my age gossiped about boys or classes before sleep, I was home in bed, reading about all of my adventures.

"I thought you said you graduated college." Lindy snuggles deeper into her cocoon of blankets.

"I did, but it was all online to get my associate's degree. I've never really grown up knowing what I wanted to do. As bad as it might sound, I've really only ever wanted to be a wife and mother, so I never saw the point in going another two years to get my bachelor's when an associate's was good enough. Guess now it's probably not." I flush in embarrassment. "I'm an idiot."

"No, you're not. Don't feel ashamed about wanting to be a mom or a wife. You want to take care of people. There's nothing wrong with that."

"Yeah, except I haven't pursued my dream wholeheartedly because I'm definitely not married with kids. My life isn't exactly turning out the way I expected. Kicked out of my parent's house. Alone."

"You're not alone. Alaska's got your back. You've got me and Caroline. Let me introduce you to her book club girls, who are a hoot. Those are three more friends to support you."

"I don't want to be a charity case..." I feel pathetic enough without people pitying me.

"Hey, don't get down on yourself. Because I get it. I'm working on my own stuff since my ex-boyfriend Dean was very controlling. I pushed away from my family and friends until I had no one. It took me a really long time to get out of that relationship, and I'm still trying to recover. We can heal together."

Hugging a decorative pillow close to my chest, gratitude slips through my veins like a calming cup of chamomile tea. "Thank you, Lindy, and I'm sorry about your ex-boyfriend."

Lindy flips through the streaming service searching for something else to watch and shrugs. "It is what it is. I just hope to never see him again... What about you with your dad? What's the story there?"

"Well, obviously, he's a pastor. He's always been very charismatic. But I think he kept his extreme views hidden while my mom was alive. After she died, it was just me and him, and it was like a switch flipped. He became even more conservative and controlling."

I remember those days when slowly my world became smaller and smaller as I grew older. "Most of the women in our congregation are expected to stay at home until they get married, then have as many children as possible. And while I stayed at home, I never got married. That's the one thing I never understood with my dad. He didn't push me onto someone at eighteen. I'm thankful for it, but I've never understood why. Maybe he just appreciated me taking care of him instead of a husband? I don't know. Anyway, I don't believe those are the only roles for a woman, if I ever truly did thanks to romance novels..."

"Meaning you'll fit right into the book club," Lindy supplies.

I smile, looking forward to discussing the books I love with fellow readers who appreciate them. "I still kind of followed along and lived that life, though."

There's a faint roar of a motorcycle outside, and I seize the opportunity to change the subject, hating how maudlin we're becoming. "Have you ridden with one of the guys yet?"

Lindy's eyes widen as she shakes her head. "Definitely not."

"Oh... I thought maybe you and Timber..."

She rolls her eyes and loudly exhales in exasperation. "You and the rest of the girls. Timber's protective, yes, but it's in his DNA. He'd be the same with any woman. It has nothing to do with me."

"Except he stands watch over your cabin, not another woman's." The giant biker can usually be found trekking around the treeline outside the cabin, keeping discreet watch over its inhabitants. I immediately noted his presence upon moving in because I almost mistook him for Nolan.

Lindy doesn't reply, instead focusing on finding another movie to start on the TV. Shrugging in acceptance, I can't resist adding one last comment before letting the topic go. "Well, whether it's with Timber or another club member, I recommend going on at least one ride on the back of their bikes. It's an experience like no other."

Freeing.

Exhilarating.

Remembering how it felt to sit behind Nolan for the first time with my arms wrapped around his firm waist sends a shiver down my body that settles between my thighs.

My date with Nolan went well. We covered the heavy topics of our fathers and our relationship before diving into lighter subjects like our favorite hobbies and whether or not a tomato really should be categorized as a fruit.

It was silly. Fun. Unlike our initial meeting that ended in a torrid affair.

No, our first official date was more than I ever imagined in all my daydreams as a teen reading Lisa Kleypas and Nora Roberts. The only slight hiccup to the evening was Nolan leaving me with a kiss at the cabin.

A totally delicious and passionate kiss.

But still just a tangling of mouths versus our bodies.

Granted, Lindy was inside the cabin, and his room at the main house wasn't exactly private with the rest of the members hanging out just outside the door, but I craved more.

However bad it made me.

Good thing Nolan likes bad girls.

Or at least punishing them.

The ghost of his hand spanking my upturned bottom trembled over my skin. Tossing my blanket aside, I sat up to chug a drink from the homemade sangrias Lindy and I whipped up.

Stop making yourself so hot!

But it was difficult when the memories bombarded me.

So do something about it. I thought about the selection of sex toys hidden in a pink box in my bedroom, wishing it was Nolan sequestered in there instead.

"Is a romantic comedy alright with you?" Lindy asks, her finger hovering over the play button.

"Sure, sounds good," I squeaked, focusing on the TV. Maybe a few good laughs would cool my hormones.

Maybe...

CHAPTER THIRTEEN

FAITH

"Welcome to The Ole Aces!" Caroline sweeps her arm out to encompass the brightly-lit bar before us. It's my first time hanging out with her book club, and I'm nervous, despite the warm greetings everyone gives me.

I've never had friends my age. It's always been Ms. Haversham and Mercy, whenever we were able to sneak a conversation in without her uncle hovering nearby.

Caroline leads the way to a corner booth inside where the six of us slide over on the vinyl seating until we're comfortably spaced around the table. A waitress quickly takes our drinks order, then Kat whips out the paperback version of the book club's reading pick.

"Alright, who's fighting me for Hex?" Kat fans herself with the book and exaggerates a swoony expression.

Laughing at her antics, some of my nerves drain away. This is familiar—falling for a fictional boyfriend—and it grounds me a little bit more. "You can have Hex. I'm holding out for Graveyard," I say, tossing out another name from the MC series we're reading.

An hour flies by as we discuss the book and down a steady flow of food and alcohol. My head is buzzing from the one margarita I consumed and the joy of hanging out with women who love what I love—reading. It feels like I've finally found a group of people who get me. The real Faith that I'm discovering more and more each day with the distance between me and Dad.

Church expectations aren't weighing on my shoulders. No one expects perfection from me, and I almost want to cry with the wave of relief it brings. I hadn't realized just how heavy the burden had become until now.

The bar doors swing open to let in more customers, but the three people who enter are a surprise. They're congregants of my dad's church: Beau, Nehemiah, and Joseph.

What are they doing here?

Their narrowed gazes scan the room with disgust before each man splits off and approaches random tables, shoving the pamphlets in their hands in front of customers.

"Oh, no..." I whisper, embarrassment rising in my chest. Nolan and Caroline mentioned the club being harassed by overzealous congregants, but this is the first time I've actually witnessed the trouble.

"What is it?" Lindy follows my horrified stare to where Beau is sternly pointing his finger at a poor patron trying to enjoy his mug of beer. "Who is that?"

"Beau."

Amalie, Kat, Beth, and Caroline twist their heads around to see who I'm talking about. "Beau as in the man your dad wanted you to marry?"

I nod in response to Caroline's question, wishing I could sink into the floor right about now. If Beau notices me, he'll report back to my father, which shouldn't bother me considering how Dad's treated me, but there's still a part of that obedient daughter inside that cringes at the thought of disappointing him.

"Are these the guys who've been calling the compound nonstop about repenting or whatever?" Kat cranes her neck past Amalie for a better view. "Why are they here instead?"

"Probably because it's well-known around town that this is the Reaper's Wolves' favorite hang-out," Caroline mutters, frantically typing on her phone. "Snow will be here soon. I let him know what's going on, though it looks like Austin's going to beat him to the punch."

A large man with scars on his face marches toward Beau, grabbing the collar of Joseph as he drags him away from another table. "This is private property, and we don't condone harassment or bigotry. You and your friends need to take your bullshit and peddle it somewhere else."

"We have a duty to educate these people, including you." Beau slams a pamphlet into Austin's chest. He must have a death wish to challenge a man twice his size with military experience to boot. I've heard all about the bar's owner and his whirlwind romance with Luna, a close friend of Caroline's, so I know Beau is hopelessly outmatched.

"Touch me again, and you'll be the one receiving an *education*. You've got thirty seconds to vacate or else I'm calling Sheriff Lawson. And trust me, He's not buddy buddy with you and your pastor. He won't hesitate to bring you in for harassment and trespassing."

Beau pales at the threat, though he tries to shrug it off. "All we're doing is having civilized conversations with these folks. Warning them about this place and your friends. We're not—" It's then that Beau spots me. "Faith? Your daddy would be ashamed to know you're here, too."

Everyone shifts their attention to me, and I stand up on shaky legs, forcing myself toward the altercation with bricks for feet. Once I'm close enough to not have to shout to be heard, I address Beau, "Dad's already ashamed of me. He's made that abundantly clear. Please leave before the law gets involved."

"You're sticking up for them?" He hitches a thumb toward Austin and a couple of Reaper's Wolves members who were sitting at the bar. Whistling low, a hardness enters his eyes. "God saved me from having you as a wife. It's obvious you're not the girl I thought you were."

Before I can respond, Beau is smashed into a nearby table. Nolan has a grip on his neck and is hunched over to growl in Beau's ear.

When did he get here?

Snow and Timber are in the background, both hovering protectively in front of Caroline and Lindy.

"That's because she's a goddamned woman, asshole. A woman meant for more than catering to your backwards beliefs and outdated hierarchies." Nolan tightens his hold on Beau who releases a pathetic whimper. This should not be making me as hot as it is, but wow... I can't take my eyes off the powerful display before me.

Nolan's arms flex with strength, causing his tattoos to dance. His large palms remind me of how he held me down during our first night together, of how it felt when he spanked me on his motorcycle. And after all the talk about fictional MC boyfriends during book club, I'm ready for my real-life biker to take me for a ride.

"She was never gonna be your wife because she belongs to me. Not because I control her or because I think she's beneath me." Nolan looks up and says the next part like he's speaking directly to my soul. "Faith is mine because I want to worship at her altar for as long as she'll have me. Because she claimed me as her own the moment I caught sight of her. Isn't that right, princess?"

Speechless by his declaration, all I can manage is a quick nod of my head and shy smile. Nolan hasn't exactly been secretive about his desire, but announcing it to a bar full of people is next level commitment.

"Princess?" Beau scoffs, ruining the moment. I forgot where we were for a second, too wrapped up in Nolan to notice Beau still flattened against the wooden grain of a bar table. "More like a whore!"

CHAPTER FOURTEEN

ALASKA

That's it.

This motherfucker deserves the beat down of his life for insulting my woman.

"What did you just call her?" I lean more of my weight on this jackass's back, crushing his nose into the tabletop. Its previous patrons disappeared right around the time I sent Beau flying forward after hearing him use *Faith* and *wife* in the same sentence.

"Come on, Alaska. Let's take this outside. We've disturbed Austin's business enough." Snow pats my shoulder before taking custody of the man Austin had restrained. "Sorry about this, brother."

"Just another typical night at The Ole Aces when it comes to you guys." Austin shakes his head with a ragged sigh. He rubs the back of his neck before lifting his chin toward the bar doors. "I'll let you deal with them while I placate any disgruntled customers."

A group of us shuffle outside, including Faith and Caroline's book club. Reluctantly, I release Beau as Timber and Snow shove his companions forward. "Get in your car and go. We don't want any more trouble."

The men retreat, the two smarter men dragging Beau with them. "This isn't over," he warns. "We've got righteousness on our side. The Lord will prevail!"

"Let's hope he prevails in knocking some sense into you," Snow mutters. He tugs Caroline close with an arm around her waist as we watch the trio pile into an old sedan and peel out of the gravel parking lot.

"I'm so sorry about this." Faith's soft voice floats on the gentle breeze blowing away the dust kicked up by Beau's vehicle. "Usually, they keep their judgments to the church groups. Rarely do they venture out for confrontations. Something about your MC has gotten them riled up like nothing I've ever seen before."

"You don't need to apologize for them. They're grown adults acting like petulant children when they don't get their way," Snow says. "Honestly, I'm glad they've chosen to focus on us rather than another group. We can handle their annoying antics without things escalating to all-out violence. Another MC like the Ghost Riders wouldn't blink an eye at shooting first and asking questions later."

"I never even considered that happening!" Distress fills her voices as she stares after the spot where we last saw Beau's car. I hate that her former church is causing her worry, but there's not much I can do to help the situation. These people refuse to listen to reason.

The women decide to end the book club early due to the incident, so Faith rides home with me on the back of my bike. But as we near the cabin she shares with Lindy, Faith taps my shoulder and points ahead toward the trail leading into the woods.

Following her silent command, I ride deeper into the forest, the moonlight dappling the ground as we come to a stop. Faith immediately hops off the bike and gives me her helmet to store.

"Feeling restless?" I ask.

"Something like that..." She bites her bottom lip. "I know I should be upset or more concerned about what happened tonight, but all I really want to do is..." She pauses and glances away. "The way you handled Beau tonight, what you said, it really affected me." Her hands wring together at her waist.

I recall claiming her again in front of everyone. Is this the part when she tells me it's too much and tries to run again?

Our date the other night went well, even if I had to force myself to leave her with only a kiss. I was trying to be a gentleman. Set us on a steady course forward that might better resemble how she imagined her life going—date and get to know a man then let him fuck her until she passed out from pleasure.

"Spit it out, princess.".

"I want to suck your cock."

Of all the things I imagined Faith saying, those six words didn't even make the top one thousand. "Excuse me?" Surely, I misheard her. Though the burgeoning hardness in my jeans seems to have heard just fine.

So much for trying to be a gentleman.

"I want to suck your cock. You didn't let me that first night we were together. When you tasted me," she pauses, and I just know there's a blush blooming on her cheeks in this darkness. "Now, I want to taste you."

She steps forward and her hands tentatively rest on the button of my jeans. "Is that okay?"

"Hell yeah, if that's what you want." I readjust on my bike, so I'm facing her fully, and help her unzip my jeans to free my rock hard cock. Pre-cum dribbles from the tip, ready for my princess to lick it up.

Eagerly, Faith goes to her knees, leaves crunching beneath the movement, silvery light shining on her blonde hair. Her plump lips tease along the length before engulfing the throbbing head, her delicate hands circling the base to squeeze.

"That's it, princess, just like that. I should've known you needed a cock stuffing that pretty mouth of yours full. My sweet dirty girl."

Her cloudy gaze meets mine as she continues to pump me with her hands and mouth, sucking me off like a good little church girl. Fuck! For a virgin at sucking cock, my woman sure knows how to make me blow quicker than a boy on prom night.

"Harder. I'm about to cum, princess."

A moan vibrates along my dick as she draws me deeper until I hit the back of her throat. Faith coughs a little, backing up, before diving back in, determined to get it right and get *me* off.

"Goddamn, you're perfect. My curvy little good girl is desperate to swallow my thick cock."

Too soon I'm exploding on her tongue, my cum splashing down her lips and chin before she wipes it off and swipes her tongue over her fingers.

"Holy hell, that's hot as fuck."

"I feel hot as fuck," she says, a satisfied smirk transforming her beautiful features.

The roar of motorcycles arriving at the compound interrupts the moment, and Faith skitters to her feet with my help. "That'll be Lindy and Timber. I should get back."

"You can't leave yet. I need another taste of your cunt." It's been almost two weeks since I ate her pussy, and that's two fucking weeks too long.

She puts a finger to my lips and shakes her head with a smile. "Not tonight, biker man. That was just for you." Then she turns and runs back toward the cabins.

Faith may be running, but this time I don't feel an emptiness when she leaves. Because I know it's not for good.

Faith's not running from me.

She's running toward her friend to make sure she's okay.

And that makes a world of difference.

CHAPTER FIFTEEN

ALASKA

"You're not gonna believe this shit." Fox enters the kitchen where we're all eating breakfast the next morning. An expression of stunned disbelief hardens his jaw. "There's a crowd of crazy churchgoers out front, and guess who's part of their congregation?"

The seven of us at the table—me, Faith, Snow, Caroline, Lindy, Timber, and Grim—share confused glances before I finally take the bait. "Who?"

"Snake, your fucking dad."

"What the hell? Are you sure?" I haven't heard from him since he showed up at the old gym. We lost track of him after the gas station incident. Never heard any rumblings from the Shadow Demons MC about joining up with him, so I'd hoped he disappeared for good. Kept on driving past Shadow Demons territory, since he'd gotten a little bit of money.

Clearly, that was too much to hope for.

"Yeah, he's out front shouting with the reverend and wearing one of those nice suits with his hair slicked back looking like a regular churchgoer."

"Seriously?" Religion and Snake don't mix. The man's ego is too big to trust a higher power. Faith's hand brushes mine under the table, and I note the compassion in her violet eyes.

It's comforting having her here, knowing she understands what I'm feeling.

Snow tosses his napkin on the table and scoots back to stand. "Guess we ought to deal with this. Can't have one peaceful morning." Caroline snags his arm and tugs him to a halt for a quick peck to his cheek. Immediately, there's a softening to our president's demeanor, and I marvel at the power of our women.

We may be military vets, motorcycle-riding club members—strong and lethal—but that's nothing compared to the strength of the women in our lives. Caroline and Faith rule quietly with gentle touches and calm encouragement.

As a group, we lumber outside to see what Fox was talking about. Sure enough, there's a crowd at the end of the compound's long drive, and my dad is shouting into a bullhorn.

"I used to be one of these heathens, but after hearing the Word from your great pastor, I changed my ways. When I tried to convince the rest of the Reaper's Wolves members to join me, they shunned me, kicked me out. Does that sound Christian to you?"

"No!" Everybody shouted.

This is fucking ridiculous.

Once they've caught sight of us, the crowd starts moving down the drive, Faith's father and mine leading the charge. Smugness radiates from the reverend, and there's Beau behind him wearing the same expression.

Assholes.

"You weren't kidding about us having similar dads," Faith whispers from my side. Her arm is looped through mine, her head resting below my shoulder.

"Thank God we're nothing like them, huh?"

Reverend Harris and my dad stop at the foot of the stairs to the compound porch—two oily snakes bent on spewing their venom. "What do you have to say for yourselves?"

"That you must be out of your fucking mind teaming up with this bastard." Snow points to Snake amid concurring grumbles from more of the club members spilling out of the main house. "He's wanted for armed robbery and was kicked out of the club due to orchestrating thefts with another motorcycle club. He's far from the repentant sinner he's portraying to you."

"Lies!" Snake yells. His hand shakes as raises the bullhorn and faces the crowd at his back. "They're trying to twist my good name!"

Members of the congregation murmur in agreement. It's a sea of pastels—lavender and pink skirt suits for the women and yellow and green polos for the men. We could be at a posh country club if it weren't for the freshly-made signs several people were holding.

Repent or Else!

Heathens are for hell!

It's some dark and twisted shit for a group ranging from the middle-aged to elderly.

Stepping forward, I address Snake, "You have some nerve coming here like this. Was this your ridiculous scheme?" My narrowed gaze travels over the crowd. "I guarantee he's figured out a way to steal from all of you. Where have your tithes been going? Are funds missing? Check your accounts because there's no doubt you've been taken in by a grifter."

"They've even turned my own son against me!" Snake shouts, although I see a couple of people starting to doubt Snake's faithfulness to their cause. *Once a devil, always a devil.* No amount of pomade and veneer can hide Snake's true colors.

A police siren wails in the background before two law enforcement vehicles pull to a stop on our drive. Sheriff Lawson exits one SUV and strides forward with purpose, straight toward my dad.

"Leroy Dallas, otherwise known as Snake." He tries to melt into the crowd, but everyone separates from him. Sheriff Lawson continues, "You're under arrest for armed robbery and thefts in Everton, High Ridge, and Suitor's Crossing."

He Mirandizes my dad then slaps cuffs onto his wrists. The congregants remain eerily silent, shocked by the turn of events. Frankly, so am I. I wonder which MC member called the cops?

"If I were you folks, I'd get out of here and check your bank accounts, your credit cards. This man is a known felon for stealing money." Lawson's words catalyze a rush to leave as everyone disappears with their tails between their legs.

The last one to go is the reverend.

He scowls at Faith, but doesn't say anything. Have we actually made him speechless? It'd be a fucking miracle.

"You should go too, Dad," Faith says, standing straighter beside me. "I'm ashamed to be your daughter." And then, like a boss, she turns around without a backward glance, the finality in her tone making me hard.

My woman finally stood up for herself. Sure, Faith left her father's house which was a great first step, but now it's clear—she's done taking her dad's bullshit.

Just like I'm taking Snake's. He'll be behind bars for who knows how long, but it doesn't matter.

I've got my girl and my club, and that's all I really need.

CHAPTER SIXTEEN

FAITH

I t was surprisingly easy letting go of my dad and the church I grew up in, especially after all the guilt and shame I've been feeling.

God loves me the way I am, and my dad doesn't.

It's as simple as that.

When I saw him standing next to Nolan's father, both of them trying to tear down their children's home and new family, it struck me how similar Nolan and I truly are. It doesn't matter if his background is in the military or a biker club, and it doesn't matter if mine was sheltered and uber conservative.

We've both dealt with trauma from our parents, but now we can move forward together. Because I'm not running from my biker anymore.

"How are you feeling?" Nolan wraps his arms around me. We're in his room in the compound for a little privacy. There's a game playing on the massive TV in the living room, its loud volume ensuring no one will bother us.

"Good... Empowered. I hope this is the end of being harassed by them." They marched on the compound with signs in hand like a freaking protest. As if the Reaper's Wolves were infringing on their rights, when the *MC* was the one being harassed.

Witnessing Beau, my dad, and even Mercy Campion who hid behind her uncle, no doubt dragged to the demonstration, had been confirmation that my old life was in the past. I could never return to the girl who silently obeyed her father. Didn't want his type of *love*.

The realization didn't leave me as lonely as before. Like Lindy said, I'm not alone. I've got a new family. A *found* family. People who genuinely care about me—not because I'm perfect or follow their rules but because of who I am as a person.

"Me, too. But even if it's not, we'll get through it."

"We will." I circle my arms around his neck and lean up for a kiss. "Nolan, I know I've apologized already, but I'm sorry I left you that first night. It was a mistake, and I promise I won't ever run again. You're stuck with me."

"That's what I like to hear." He grins before tossing me onto his bed. Technically, I shouldn't be tossable, but he's so big and strong that even a plus-size girl like me feels tiny in comparison.

I giggle as he tickles my stomach, then moan in pleasure as he changes tactics, kissing me hard, his hand massaging my hip.

"I adore you, princess. Nothing's gonna get between us. Not your dad, not mine, nothing." He stops long enough to stare down at me, letting me see how serious he is.

"I know... It's my prayer every night," I confess. Sometimes I'm afraid this is an elaborate dream I'll wake up from. A manifestation of my immense romance reading. Because who would have thought a church mouse like me would land a sexy biker like Nolan?

"You still pray? But you're a heathen now like the rest of us." He jokes, and I roll my eyes.

"Time to prove your *devilish* ways," I tease, tossing my hands over my head and wriggling my hips beneath his. The thick, hard length of his cock rubs against the seam of my jeans, and I want it. Now.

"So cock hungry, my little princess," Nolan tsks with a wink. Quickly, he rids us of our clothing until we're lying naked chest to chest. It's been forever since I've felt the wiry hair on his chest rasping across my nipples. Reveled in the heat of his skin burning into mine.

Time to make up for lost time.

"I'm hungry for *you*."

A rumbling growl is Nolan's response as he licks a path between my breasts. They overflow his large palms, creating a deep valley that he's nestling in. "One of these days I'm going to fuck these sexy tits of yours. Slide between their soft bounty until I paint these puffy pink nipples with my cum."

His tongue circles my areola. Round and round. Taunting me by avoiding the sensitive tip.

My fingers dive into his shaggy hair and lightly pull. "Stop teasing and fuck me," I order, the curse falling freely when Nolan has me worked up like this. It's like my filter evaporates once all the blood begins pulsing in my clit.

Nolan slaps the back of my thigh where my leg is wrapped around his waist. "You're not in charge, princess. I decide how to fuck you. Soft, slow, hard, fast. It's all up to me. Your only job is to lie back like a good girl and accept whatever I give you."

I'd forgotten he was like this our first night at the hotel, too. Dominant. Alpha. Another rush of arousal dripped between my thighs.

"Is that clear?" Nolan moves down my body and nips my belly before using both of his hands to spread my legs apart, forcing my heels to drop to the bed. I'm wide open for his perusal, and there's a slight stretch in my muscles at the exposed position.

"Are you searching for a *yes, sir*?" I hadn't been this sassy our first time, overwhelmed with sensations. But I know Nolan better now. Know *myself* better now. And the woman I'm becoming enjoys teasing her man.

"That'll do..." He swipes his tongue from my clenching pussy to my clit, and I arch at the sudden contact, seeking more. But Nolan moves upward again so his mouth hovers over mine, fitting the tip of his dick at my entrance. "I'll also accept an enthusiastic *amen*."

My surprised laughter transforms into a high-pitched gasp as he plunges deep. Every inch of him stretching my pussy in one fell swoop. Despite my vibrators and dildos, Nolan's cock is the biggest thing to ever fuck me. Thick and long with a flared head, it hits every erogenous spot perfectly. Like he was made just for me.

Or I was made for him.

His hips rear back and begin a pounding rhythm, driving me further up the mattress until my head cracks against the headboard, and he swiftly apologizes, placing a hand there to protect me.

"God, how do you feel this *good*? So perfect? This pussy's even better than I remember, and I didn't think I'd forgotten a single detail." Nolan grunts, sweat darkening the hair at his temples. "Touch yourself, princess. Pet that pretty little clit and soak my dick with your cream."

Who am I to disobey my man?

With one hand, I pull him in for a kiss while the other skates between our damp bodies until I find my clit, eager for more direct stimulation. The added effort doesn't go unnoticed because soon my body tenses before exploding around Nolan's cock.

"Fuck!" He shouts, pumping once, twice then stilling as his release fills me up with thick ropes of cum. Nolan collapses to the side but retains a hold on me, his hand cupping my hip to drag me closer.

I feel replete. Satisfied. Relaxed. Even if we forgot to use protection.

We. Forgot. To. Use. Protection.

Twisting my head, I look at Nolan. "You didn't wear a condom."

"Oh, shit." Realization dawns as he glances down at his semi-hard cock. As if one will materialize. "I'm clean. Obviously. Haven't been with anyone since you. But a baby... Is that something you want?"

I turn to my side to face him and nod, shy all of a sudden. "Yes. Eventually. I've always wanted to be a wife and mom, just not how my dad envisioned I should be." There's actually a bit of shame about yearning for such simple things—things my dad wanted for me, too.

"The difference is you understand those aren't the only value you have," Nolan says, knowing the exact thing to help ease my shame. "When and if you get pregnant, I'm not going anywhere. I'm here for you and any babies. I've got to break the generational curse of our fathers, after all."

"You don't have to worry about acting like them." I cup his bearded cheek and smile. "You're a good man. Kind. So far from them that it's never even entered my mind to be concerned about potential children and you."

"That's a lot of trust to put in me."

"You've earned it." And he has. From rescuing me from No Man's Land to helping me move out of my dad's house. Even handling Beau at The Ole Aces.

Nolan's proven he's solid, trustworthy.

A dangerous, giant biker on the outside—my large teddy bear on the inside. I'm falling for him with every chat, kiss, touch we share. And I tell him so, tired of keeping my feelings bottled up.

Nolan grins. "Baby, I think I've loved you from the moment I got lost in those pretty violet eyes." He rolls over to kiss me again, and I melt in his embrace.

No more words needing to be spoken.

EPILOGUE

FAITH

The bell rings at Dusty's as my husband comes in with a proud smile.

"It's finished."

"Really?" I hold myself up from the desk chair, pressing a hand to my back as my round belly compresses all my organs. I can't wait until this baby is out. Pregnancy was fun when the extra hormones made me a sex addict that Nolan did his best to satisfy. But now I'm toddling around on swollen feet, and it sucks.

Though I guess I shouldn't complain too much.

Nolan and I have been together for a year, and everything else has been pure bliss.

Dad and my former church stopped harassing the club after finding out they were taken in by Snake for thousands of dollars. I like to think embarrassment keeps them from coming by anymore. Humiliation for falling for a conman's game.

Nolan and I got married six weeks after we first met, which is when he started building our own cabin on the compound. It's close to where the trail begins, the special place we always escape to for privacy.

"It's done. Grim, Timber, and I spent the morning moving the furniture in, so we can finally sleep there tonight."

"I can't wait!" I'm ready to nest in our own home before the baby comes—something that's difficult to do in the temporary apartment we leased once we were married.

Rather than returning to Alaska, Nolan manages the renovated club gym, while I still work at Dusty's. But when the baby arrives, I'll be taking a long maternity leave and only working part-time as needed, so I'm searching for a replacement.

Working and earning my own money has been a confidence booster, but in the end, I truly do only want to be a mother and wife. I want to be there for my babies. For all of their firsts. And I want to welcome Nolan home every evening.

Simple pleasures. But ones I'm immensely grateful for.

To think, it all started with a trip outside my comfort zone...

CHAPTER ONE

AMELIE

I 've got a secret—a naughty, sexy hidden life.

One my best friends don't even know about.

The beginning strains of "Desperado" by Rihanna swells from the stage, and that's my cue. Sauntering into the spotlight, I exaggerate the sway of my hips and offer a little shimmy of my chest to the crowd of men gathered around the edges of the raised platform.

Amelie Swanson would never perform at a strip club. She's too shy, self-conscious... too *good*. But Velvet Venus? She's a *bad girl*, a *dangerous woman*. Confident and sultry, she thrives on teasing men.

To a point.

I don't strip to nothing, even that's too wild for my alter ego, but burlesque is all about the mystery—revealing bits and pieces of bare skin to drive the audience to distraction. The art of it has fascinated me ever since watching the movie Burlesque and desperately wishing to be Christina Aguilera's character. A woman who escaped her small town for the big city and found her dream job.

While this isn't exactly my dream job, it's definitely a side hustle that brings me happiness. Men never salivate over chubby little Amelie. I'm overlooked or ignored. However,

Velvet Venus never enters a room without drawing every eye to her lush curves and coy smile. It's an intoxicating feeling.

My song fades out, and I take one last bow, shaking my glitter-fringed boy shorts and bra, having lost the layers of clothing I started with. Raucous applause erupts as some men shout for me to take it all off. Leaving them with a saucy wink, I ignore their pleas and skip backstage where the next woman is preparing to step out.

"You were great out there!" Luxe says, grinning in anticipation of her own set.

"Thank you! They're all yours."

The path to a communal dressing room is clogged with racks of sparkling costumes, stagehands, and more performers. It's a real production for Club Wolf's Burlesque Night, a weekly show for men and women alike.

Every other evening men can watch the regular exotic dancers strip bare but not tonight. This is a specialty event created by one of the co-managers of the club, Stacy. She runs it with a member of the Reaper's Wolves MC—the motorcycle club who owns Club Wolf.

Which means my hidden hobby sits precariously close to being found out now that friends of mine are loved-up with Reaper's Wolves members. But I couldn't resist the temptation of trying burlesque when they first announced the weekly event. And now I'm a headliner!

There's freedom in having this one thing for myself. Not that I don't trust my friends or believe they'll support me. Because they one-hundred percent will. But no one knowing my secret means there's no pressure to act a certain way—to be Amelie versus Venus.

They're two sides of the same person but only one gets to see the light of day.

Maybe someday I'll feel comfortable enough revealing this naughtier side of me. *Preferably with a hot man who adores me no matter what.* But until then, I'll disappear to Club Wolf every Tuesday night and dance to my heart's content with no one the wiser.

Not my family.

Not my friends.

No one.

Find out what happens next in *Grim's Goddess*!

THANKS FOR READING & DON'T FORGET TO RATE/ REVIEW!

Please consider leaving a rating/review. Ratings & reviews are the #1 way to support an indie author like me.
I appreciate your support!
XO, Hallie

ABOUT THE AUTHOR

Hallie prefers steamy, insta-love stories where curvy girls are claimed by filthy-talking heroes. And when she ran out of reading material, she decided to write her own stories. If you want a quick, hot read, she's your girl!

www.ingramcontent.com/pod-product-compliance
Lightning Source LLC
Chambersburg PA
CBHW030351180626
46812CB00007B/2839